I Was a
Teenage Fairy

Also by Francesca Lia Block

Weetzie Bat

Witch Baby

Cherokee Bat and the Goat Guys

Missing Angel Juan

Baby Be-Bop

Girl Goddess #9: *Nine Stories*

The Hanged Man

Dangerous Angels:
The Weetzie Bat Books

Francesca Lia Block

I Was a
Teenage Fairy

Joanna Cotler Books
An Imprint of HarperCollins*Publishers*

Library of Congress Cataloging-in-Publication Data
Block, Francesca Lia.
    I was a teenage fairy / by Francesca Lia Block.
        p.   cm.
    "Joanna Cotler books."
    Summary: A feisty, sexy fairy helps a young girl heal traumas of her
past.
    ISBN 0-06-027747-5. — ISBN 0-06-027748-3 (lib. bdg.)
    [1. Fairies—Fiction.   2. Child sexual abuse—Fiction.   3. Los Angeles
(Calif.)—Fiction.]   I. Title.
PZ7.B61945Iae   1998   98-14598
[Fic]—dc21   CIP
                                                                      AC

Designed by Christine Kettner
1   2   3   4   5   6   7   8   9   10
❖
First Edition

For my three fairy queens
Gilda, Joanna, Lydia

PART I

Barbie & Mab

If Los Angeles is a

woman reclining billboard model with collagen-puffed lips and silicone-inflated breasts, a woman in a magenta convertible with heart-shaped sunglasses and cotton candy hair; if Los Angeles is this woman, then the San Fernando Valley is her teeny-bopper sister. The teenybopper sister snaps big stretchy pink bubbles over her tongue and checks her lip gloss in the rearview mirror, causing Sis to scream. Teeny plays the radio too loud and bites her nails, wondering if the glitter polish will poison her. She puts her bare feet up on the dash to admire her tan legs and the blond hair that is so pale and soft she doesn't have to shave. She wears a Val Surf T-shirt and boys' boxer shorts and she has a boy's phone

3

number scrawled on her hand. Part of her wants to spit on it and rub it off, and part of her wishes it was written in huge numbers across her belly, his name in gang letters, like a tattoo. The citrus fruits bouncing off the sidewalk remind her of boys; the burning oil and chlorine, the gold light smoldering on the windy leaves. Boys are shooting baskets on the tarry playground and she thinks she can smell them on the air. And in her pocket, whispering secrets about them, is a Mab.

Maybe Mab was real. Maybe there really are girls the size of pinkies with hair the color of the darkest red oleander blossoms and skin like the greenish-white underbellies of calla lilies.

Maybe not. Maybe Mab was the fury. Maybe she was the courage. Maybe later on she was the sex. But it doesn't matter if Mab is real or imagined, Barbie thought, as long as I can see her. As long as I can feel her sitting on my palm, ticklish as a spider, as long as I can hear the cricket of her voice. Because without her then how would I be able to ever go inside?

Inside was carpeted in shag—lime green and baby blue, scratchy and synthetic, creeping insidiously over the floors and even up onto the sink counters and toilet seats in the bathroom. It was a kitchen with cows stenciled on the walls and real cows roasting in the oven. It was pictures of Barbie's mother when she was a young beauty queen contestant and model, flashing big teeth like porcelain bullets. It was Barbie's mother now, jingling with gold chains and charms, big-haired, frosted, loud enough to scare away even the bravest pinkie-sized girls.

Sometimes Barbie's mother came outside, too, to yank her daughter by one skinny arm from under a bush and pull leaves out of hair that was green from swimming too long in the chlorinated pool.

That day, Barbie had been lying there calling for Mab who was being especially obstinate and refusing to make an appearance.

"Barbie! We're going to be late! What are you doing?"

Barbie's mother was wearing her oversized white plastic designer sunglasses and a gold and white outfit. Her perfume made Barbie's head spin in a different and more nauseating way than when she and Mab attempted to get a buzz from sniffing flowers or when they spun in circles to make themselves dizzy.

"Oh my God! You're a mess! And we have to be there in forty-five minutes."

"Where?" Barbie asked her mother's tanned cleavage as she was dragged into the avocado-colored stucco house for grooming.

The agency was over the canyon in Beverly Hills. It had high ceilings, vast glass walls and enormous artwork depicting lipsticks and weapons. To Barbie, it seemed like a palace for the Giants. The Giants were the ones she had nightmares about. It was not that she was so afraid of them hurting her. The thing that made her wake sweating and biting herself with terror was that in the dream she was huge and heavy and bloated and tingling and thick.

She was one of them.

The agency was where the Giants would live.

Barbie wished Mab had come with her. But Mab never left the backyard. She said she was afraid of getting squashed. Barbie assumed that the fact Mab never went anywhere with her was proof that Mab was probably real. Otherwise, Barbie would definitely have imagined her here now.

The agent had a stretched, tanned face, like a saddle.

"Well, you certainly are pretty, Barbie," he said.

"Thank you," said Barbie's mother.

"What do you think of a career in modeling?"

"She's thrilled. She wants to be just like Mommy."

Barbie had noticed the plant when she walked in. It was the only thing in the glass and metal room that she wanted to touch. She got up and went over to it; she always examined plants. You never knew—maybe there were more girls like Mab waiting to be discovered, and in this case, rescued.

"You know I won Miss San Fernando Valley in 19 . . . well let's just say, I was a winner! Not that you'd guess it now!" Barbie's mother patted her hairdo and eyed the agent hopefully.

Barbie patted the agent's plant. There were no Mabs on it. But even Mabless, it was the most friendly thing in the room.

"Well, you certainly have a very lovely daughter, Mrs. Markowitz."

"Marks," said Barbie's mother.

Barbie, still stroking a leaf, turned to look at her.

"What's that?" asked the agent.

"Mrs. Marks."

"I thought it said . . ." The agent spryly shuffled some papers on his desk. He had long, tan, hairy arms and surprisingly small wrists for a medium-sized man.

"That was a typo," Mrs. Marks said. She noticed Barbie and her plant. "What are you doing over there! Come sit back down."

Barbie obediently left her Mabless plant friend and went back to her chair. Mrs. Marks (Marks? Barbie thought) folded her hands tightly in her lap, wiggled her rear end into the chair and glared at her daughter. Barbie folded her hands and wiggled her rear. Mrs. Marks smiled at the agent. Barbie smiled.

The plant, which had never seen a Mab, let alone been examined for one or housed one in its leaves, might have sighed silently from its corner when Barbie Markowitz-now-Marks left.

⌒⌒

"Why'd you tell him our last name was
Marks?"

They were driving home through the canyon in the baby-blue Cadillac. Even without
Mab's prompting, Barbie occasionally felt brave
enough to speak up. Not that Mab would have
considered that question speaking up.

"Because it is, now," said Mrs. Marks. "We
need a proper stage name. I knew when I
married your father"—she always said "your
father" like it was some form of misbehavior
Barbie had visited on her—"I should have
kept my maiden name. I think that
Markowitz business ruined my career."

Barbie leaned out the window of the car,
staring at the ornately flowering trees. They
seemed almost artificial, like her mother's
flower arrangements, but she knew they were
real.

"Just don't mention this name thing to him
yet."

Barbie was still thinking about the trees.
That was another reason she believed in Mab.
Purple flowering trees seemed impossibly
beautiful, too.

"Now all we need is to get you some nice head shots. Won't that be fun."

Barbie didn't say anything. She was wishing for one of the blossoms to bring home to Mab.

"We're going to go to a very famous photographer. Are you listening? Barbie!"

Barbie looked back at her mother. Why was it called a head *shot*, she wondered.

Mrs. Marks stopped at a light. Barbie slipped out of her seat belt, got onto her knees, and reached toward one of the trees that was dangling its flowers down to her. Her mother pulled her back.

"What are you doing? Get in here!"

But Barbie had managed to snag a purple flower. She hid it in her pocket. It might make a nice hat for Mab. Barbie wished she could take photos of Mab instead of having to have them taken of her. Mab was the natural born star.

Dr. Markowitz left for work early every morning and came back late in the evening. Sometimes he ate dinner with Barbie and her mother, but mostly he ate alone in the kitchen after she was supposed to be in bed. Barbie would sneak downstairs and watch him through the crack in the door. He had probably been a handsome man at one time. Now he was losing his hair and he had a worried look under his glasses. Barbie had memories of him taking her into his office and reading her stories from his books of myths. But that was before. Now he hardly noticed her.

That night he was home early. Barbie arranged her food into a miniature landscape with salad trees and mashed potato mountains, hoping he would notice, if not her artistic abilities, then at least her poor table manners.

Mrs. Marks had not even noticed about the table manners. She was always in a better mood when Barbie's father was home—at first, anyway. "You should have seen our little miss today," she said to him.

Barbie's father did not respond. He was carefully chewing his food. Each chew was almost like a wince.

"I think we're going to have a little model on our hands."

No response still.

"Aren't you going to say anything?"

"That's very nice," said Barbie's father.

Barbie wondered what he was thinking about. One of his patients? Another little girl who played with her food and imagined grasshopper-sized playmates in the garden?

"Daddy, are you going to change your name now too?"

"What's that?"

Mrs. Marks tinkled gold charms like scales and looked as if she was going to breathe fire— some kind of dragon. "Oh, nothing."

"Don't tell me you're starting that again."

"Have you ever heard of a supermodel with the last name Markowitz? There's Shalom Harlow, but she's not Jewish. It was some hippie thing her parents did."

"You're going to give your daughter an identity crisis."

"You're the psychiatrist," Barbie's mother said. "You should know that people with funny names have a much harder time in life."

"Funny names. Yes. Like Fat Burns or Beverly Hills or Snow White. Not my father's name. Not Markowitz."

Barbie was a little glad about the name now. At least it was making her father talk.

"You're the one who insisted on Barbie," he said to Barbie's mother.

"I'd like to be Snow White," Barbie said, making potatoes into a castle.

Her mother looked over at her. "Stop playing with your food, Barbie."

Barbie folded her hands in her lap. Her father got up from the table and walked out. It was always a risk to get him to talk. Usually, when you thought of something that did, it also made him want to leave.

"See what you started," Mrs. Marks said. "Now eat your dinner." She took a forkful of brisket and jabbed it into her mouth.

Something like this had happened just before Barbie found Mab for the first time. Her mother had taken her to the beauty parlor for a "makeover" that day, and her father was angry. At first Barbie was glad that at least he had noticed. But when he left the dinner table she wasn't so sure.

"She looks like a child prostitute," she had heard him saying to her mother later that night through the wall of her room.

To comfort herself Barbie had taken out the book of photographs by the two girls holding glowing lights in their palms. It was her favorite book. The photographs had been called frauds, but Barbie was sure that they were authentic. She only wished you could make out the little fuzzy winged blurs in the girls' hands better.

"Barbie! I hope you've got that light out!" her mother had yelled through the door.

Barbie put the book under her bed, turned off the light, slid off the mattress onto her knees and prayed to the wishbone-sized girl she always dreamed of.

"Please let me see you. I think I really need to see you."

She woke later to a strange, high-pitched sound. It took her a while to realize that it was a voice, singing.

"Over hill over dale
through brush through briar
over park over pale
through flood through fire . . ."

A tiny bead of light was flickering over the ceiling like a dewdrop ready to splash from a leaf. Barbie jumped out of bed. The light flew out the window. Barbie ran to the sill and looked into the garden, where the pool was glowing like a sapphire, casting its blue light over the cricket-humming grass.

Barbie did not stop to put on her shoes. She tiptoed barefoot through the dark house, imagining the shag carpet swallowing her up, the overstuffed cushions suffocating her, the framed photographs of her young beauty-queen mother shattering into angry fragments.

Finally she managed to noiselessly slide open the glass door and run down the green Astroturf steps into the blue garden. She flung herself onto her belly and whispered into the rosebush.

"Please come out. I know you're there."

There was a rustling. Barbie jumped up. But it was only a blue cat running across the yard. And not even a truly blue cat, just the plain white kind glamorized by light.

Barbie sighed and lay on her back on the damp lawn, not caring that her pajamas were getting soaked through and that her feet and hands were numbing with cold. They were probably truly blue—not just lit that way. She looked up at the sky, which was only an empty haze, not the color of night skies in books—black or purple—not even a color you could describe at all. In the Valley, because of the smog and the city lights, you could hardly ever see stars.

Why do I think I can see her? Barbie asked herself. When I can't even see a star to wish on.

And then, just as she thought it, there was a star. Or something that looked like one, but more like a nursery-rhyme star than the real thing. And tiny. It came closer and closer—will-o'-the-wisp-ish—flitted, lit, finally, in Barbie's palm. And then the light began to change. First Barbie noticed the two slanted green eyes and then the poison-flower-red hair, then the long slender greeny-silver arms and legs, the hands with long fingers, the mouth like a miniature lipstick ad—except that when it opened the incisors were sharp and pointed, almost as if they had been filed that way. The light was not a light at all but a teenage girl-thing who was the size of most teenage girl's littlest fingers. All that was left of her original amorphous form were the incandescent wings that sprouted from her shoulder blades.

"Oh!" Barbie said.

"Is that all you can say? 'Oh!'" It was the same voice, Barbie was sure, that she had heard singing in her room. It sounded petulant now. An eye-rolling voice, a pouty-lipped voice.

"I'm sorry," Barbie stammered. "You're just so . . ."

She knew she was making things worse.

"So! So what?"

"Tiny."

Worse and worse.

"Thanks a lot." The girl looked like she were about to spit venom.

"And you have wings," Barbie said, trying hard. Gorgeous, ephemeral, shiveringly exquisite wings, was what she meant to say, but it was hard to talk at all.

"How observant!" snipped girl-thing.

"And you're so . . ."

"Beautiful," she helped out.

"Yes," breathed Barbie. Beautiful wasn't even close. There weren't words, really—none she knew of anyway—to describe.

"That's more like it. You know, you should be very grateful that you get to see me at all."

Grateful was another one, like beautiful. It didn't express what she was feeling. She wanted to squeeze the thing to let it know, but she was afraid she would crush it. She wondered if it would leave a greenish stain like bug blood.

"I am!" she said. Grateful. "Thank you so much!" She was curious about the color of its blood but instead she asked, "What's your name?"

"Mab."

"That's pretty." It sounded vaguely familiar, like something she might have seen in one of her father's books.

"It's a queen's name."

"Are you a queen?"

"Of course."

"Who are you queen of?" Barbie asked, hoping there were more—a whole army of them to fight away annoying mothers and entice distracted fathers.

Mab didn't seem to like the inquiry. "What kind of question is that?"

"Well, if you're a queen . . . I mean, I wondered if there are more of you." She thought she shouldn't mention her motives in asking yet.

But Mab seemed to find offense in almost anything anyway. "Of course there are more of me. What do you think I am? Some kind of freak of nature?"

"I didn't mean that."

"Well, what did you mean?"

"I'd just like to meet more of you is all."

"Well, aren't you greedy."

"I'm sorry."

"And stop saying you're sorry. You need to learn to stand up for yourself. But you can't meet any more of me. That's out of the question."

"Why?" Barbie asked, hopeful now, at least, that Mab had friends in the world. It would be too weird to be the only one of a kind. That was how Barbie felt herself, sometimes.

"Because . . ." Mab's voice changed for a second—a little hoarser, although the word hoarse wasn't quite right for something so minuscule. "Well, because I don't know where they are."

"I'm sorry," Barbie said, thinking about Mab trying to look for others like her on all the plants in the neighborhood. It would be much harder for her than for Barbie, Mab being that small and all, even with the help of her wings. And the wings looked more pretty than functional.

Barbie wondered if Mab could read minds. She was giving her a venomous look. Then Barbie realized she had said "sorry" again.

"Sorry."

"Would you stop! Let's just drop the whole subject."

And then before you could say her one-syllable name, she was gone in a quiversome twinkle. Quiversome was the only way to describe it, Barbie thought, wondering if that were a real word.

"Come back! I'm not sorry! Please come back! Mab."

She was suddenly aware of how cold she was again—she had forgotten it in the imaginary warmth of Mab's shimmer. Shivering, she looked up at her window where a light had gone on.

Her mother pulled back the curtains and leaned out.

"Barbie! Is that you out there? What do you think you're doing?"

Barbie's heart felt as small as Mab's pinkie. She wondered if she would ever find her again.

Hamilton Waverly had cadaver-pale skin and a fleshy mouth. He was balding but wore his scraggly dyed-black hair long to his shoulders. He made Barbie feel queasy when he looked at her, the way she felt when her mother made her eat chopped liver, or even when she smelled it. But there was something so soft about his voice and he never took his eyes off her. She wished her father paid that kind of attention. This man seemed to genuinely like her, and she didn't want to hurt his feelings.

Still, when he began to take the pictures, Barbie felt as stiff as the doll she had been named for. Her mother stood behind Hamilton Waverly making faces at her, telling her to smile.

"I think she might be more comfortable without an audience," Hamilton Waverly said. He had a long upper lip and a very slight, barely detectable lisp.

Mrs. Marks fanned herself with her long red acrylic fingernails. "She's got to get used to being watched. Besides, I'm her mother."

"Exactly," said Hamilton Waverly. "Why don't you go downstairs to the café for a little while."

"I'd prefer to stay."

"And I'd prefer if you leave." His voice sounded deeper, commanding. "I can't concentrate."

Barbie's mother stood up, straightened her chartreuse-green suit, and huffed out. Hamilton Waverly went over and knelt beside Barbie. He smelled of chemicals and something a little too sweet.

"How are you today, Barbie?" he asked gently. He really did seem to want to know.

"Okay," she said. Outside, one sickly-looking tree was tapping against the window as if it wanted to get in. Barbie wondered if any Mabs would inhabit a tree like that, this far downtown. They would be tough junkie urban Mabs, not Valley girls who got to live on honeysuckle and wear jacaranda blossoms. Barbie would have to remind Mab of how lucky she was the next time Mab complained. And maybe, Barbie thought, I'm lucky too. I have a mother who wants to make me a star. That isn't so bad, is it?

"You're a very pretty little girl," Hamilton Waverly said.

Barbie saw nothing about herself that was pretty, let alone model material. Her eyes seemed too round and her nose too small and her mouth too big. Her neck seemed too long and her elbows and knees too bony and her hair was green from the chlorine in the pool and her shoulders were peeling with sunburn. Besides, she didn't want to be a model. If anything, she would have liked to learn how the cameras worked, to stare through the lens at a little world of her own making and then capture it. She would have especially liked to learn how to take pictures of Mab and wondered if Mab photographed better than the winged girls in her favorite book.

"Aren't you going to thank me?" Hamilton Waverly tucked one stray hair behind Barbie's ear.

"Thank you." She was still staring at one of the cameras. "How does it work?"

"Do you want to look through it?" He took her hand and led her over to the camera.

In her father's book there was a Giant who had one big eye. The Cyclops. The hero had had to blind it. From behind, without the eye, the camera was less threatening. Hamilton Waverly held Barbie up and she looked through the lens. Now she was the Giant. But she didn't feel the heavy tingling numbness so she wasn't afraid. She felt almost powerful.

"Can I take your picture?"

Hamilton Waverly laughed. It was loud and startling compared to his soft stuffed-animal voice. "Not today. But next time if you're a very, very good little girl I'll let you *look*."

There was something about the way he said the last word that gave Barbie the liver feeling again. She was glad when he put her down. It was even okay to have him take her picture after that. At least he wasn't touching her with his hands. But the Cyclops eye seemed like it could drill a hole right through her, so that in the pictures the tree tapping the window would show up where her heart was supposed to be.

On the way home, Barbie thought about Mab. She had considered telling her about the tree and how Mab should be grateful to be living in suburbia with a whole pool basically to herself—even if she hated the smell of chlorine—and a lawn—even though she said it looked like the Astroturf stairs. But after being with Hamilton Waverly for an hour, Barbie was just glad to be going home to her crabbily delightful friend. She wanted to give Mab something. A present.

That night, Barbie snuck down the stairs

into the living room. The swag lamps swayed ominously, their chains casting shadows over Barbie's arms. The chandelier bluely reflected the tinkling pool light. Sometimes Barbie imagined, if there were an earthquake, how dangerous the chandelier would be with all its dangling weapons.

Emily was in her green-iron dome-shaped cage, watching Barbie with one bright bead eye on the side of her head. She cocked a question as if she were about to give her mistress away with a chirp, but Barbie shushed her and she obeyed. She even stayed silent while Barbie took the cage off its hook and went out into the garden. Maybe Emily knew that her days as a caged creature were finally coming to a close.

Barbie had thought of releasing the parakeet many times. But the deciding factor, even with the certainty of a mother's wrath, had been the photo session. In one of the photos, Hamilton Waverly had perched Barbie on a rung inside a large bird cage, and the trapped feeling it caused was enough to make her reconsider her pet's situation. Also, there was the possibility of giving the cage to Mab as a present—not to confine her there, of course, just as a place for her to play, a sort of summer guest cottage.

She opened the tiny door and the bird stepped out onto her finger. Its tiny claws reminded Barbie of Mab's slightly long toenails. It looked at her, hesitated only briefly, and then flew away. Barbie hoped it would find a whole flock of other escaped or freed domestic birds somewhere in the valley. At least the chances of that happening were better than the chance of Mab finding more girls like her. And after being inside a cage, Barbie was sure the risk was worth it.

"Mab!" Barbie called softly, peeking under the rosebush. The roses nodded their heads at her with languor as if to say, *Don't disturb us it's late we're getting our beauty sleep.* They were wickedly lovely in the darkness. Everything seemed lovelier outside, Barbie thought. Even the bird cage. It looked like a miniature garden gazebo for a girl in a story.

"Look what I brought you."

Barbie didn't see Mab moonbathing on a rose leaf behind her, with a rose petal for shade. Even if she had, she wouldn't have noticed the scowl on Mab's face, hidden by a petal moon-bonnet.

"Wouldn't it be a cute house? We can re-
decorate it any way you want."

"You have got to be kidding," said the voice
from the rosebush, as if the wicked lovelies
were actually speaking.

"There you are!" Barbie turned to see Mab
who flew off the bush, hovering just out of
reach.

"If you think that I am going to let you
lock me up in some . . ."

"Oh, I wouldn't lock you up. Cages are
awful. You could just stay in it when you
wanted."

"Stay in it! In a bird cage. Where a smelly
little pigeon . . ."

"Parakeet!" Barbie corrected. She personally
found pigeons rather frightening—rubbery
feathery varmints.

Mab didn't seem to have a much better
impression of Emily. "Oh, excuse me—parakeet.
That makes all the difference."

Barbie looked up into the starless, parakeet-
less sky. "Emily was a parakeet, and I wish I
hadn't let her go now."

"Well, it's a good thing you did."

"Really?"

"Of course. Nothing should be caged.

Especially not me. I'm telling you, for someone with such a large head you aren't very intelligent."

"Do I have a large head?" Barbie asked. Obviously in comparison to Mab's head, but maybe Mab meant too large for Barbie's body.

"Enormous. Elephantine. Bulbous."

"Do you think it's too big for modeling?"

"Absolutely." Mab spun in the air, so fast she was like a frothy milk shake of light.

"Good. Because I don't want to be a model anyway."

"You wouldn't make a good model. Look how big and clumsy you are."

Barbie stared down at her feet. She thought of the Giants. To Mab she must be like one. She wondered if she sickened Mab the way the Giants sickened her.

"My mom wants me to be."

"That horrible screeching woman. Just tell her to leave you alone."

"I can't," Barbie said. "She just wants us to have nice things and attention and stuff."

It was only when Mab said things like that, that Barbie wanted to defend her mother. Mab stopped whirring, as if someone had switched off the milk shake blender, and rolled her candy-sprinkle-green eyes.

"You're hopeless. I'm leaving."

"Don't go! Don't you want to go inside your new house?" Barbie hadn't even had the chance to tell Mab about Hamilton Waverly's cage. Then Mab might have believed that Barbie had no intention of keeping her, or anyone else, locked up.

In ballet that day Barbie had been chastised by the teacher, Madame Molotov. She had not been concentrating on the exercises and Madame had tapped her cane on the wooden floor until clouds of rosin rose up, and shouted into Barbie's ear, "Arms in fifth! Fifth!"

Barbie put her hands into first position. "Fifth!"

Barbie stuck her arms straight up in the air, as if she were being held at gunpoint, which is what it was like when Madame wielded her cane.

"Stop! Stop!" shouted Madame Molotov.

The accompanist stopped playing.

"Everyone, I'd like you to look at this young lady's idea of fifth position."

The girls in their black leotards, pink tights, and pink slippers giggled. What made the whole thing worse was that her mother had seen. Barbie stared at her feet, hating her slippers. At least if leather were dyed brown or black it didn't look so much like a dead animal's wrinkled skin.

Madame Molotov roughly forced Barbie's arms into place above her head and tapped her cane again as if she were trying to raise dead ballerinas from graves beneath the floorboards. The sight of their phantom faces might have made her feel less ancient.

It was only that Barbie was thinking about Mab. About how, for Mab, ballet would have been a breeze—literally. Mab could have stunned them all with her gravity-defying *pirouettes* and *tour jetés*. No one would have ever laughed at Barbie again if they could see who her friend Mab was. But was Mab her friend? She hadn't seen her since the parakeet/pigeon incident.

After class, Mrs. Marks was fuming. It was a hot day and she had started to perspire, releasing fumes of hair spray, antiperspirant, and perfume. She was fanning herself with her fingernails, like an overgrown bleach-blond Caucasian geisha girl.

"I'm getting a little sick of your mistakes, to tell you the truth. You have to start concentrating on things."

That was when she noticed that the bird cage was missing.

"What . . . Oh my God! Barbie, go check if the TV is still there."

Barbie thought it was a little strange that her mother would send her to check for stolen goods with the possibility of a thief still at large in the house. She imagined Giant's hands clad in ballet-slipper-pink leather gloves clapping over her mouth.

Of course, the TV was still there, as was everything else except for the bird cage.

"Yes," Barbie said.

"Yes, what?"

"It's still there."

"Why would someone just take a bird cage?" Mrs. Marks wondered aloud. "Maybe it was one of those insane animal rights people."

She went upstairs. Barbie followed her.

In the peach-and-gold bedroom, Mrs. Marks began opening drawers and pulling out velvet jewelry boxes. It seemed that all of her heavy golden chains and charms were still there.

"Nothing else is missing. Isn't that strange?"

Barbie found a rhinestone necklace and held it up in a beam of sunlight from the window. The teardrop-shaped glass cast shiny dancing sparks onto the ceiling, very much like Mab's light. This made Barbie miss Mab even more. The bird cage fiasco had fanned the flames of mother-wrath, and lost her one parakeet as expected, but it had also caused a Mab disappearance.

It really did look like a gazebo to me, Barbie thought.

"I'm speaking to you, young lady."

Barbie was still entranced by the Mabish lights.

"I've had enough for one day. Go to your room and don't bother coming down till tomorrow," her mother said.

"You spotted snakes with double tongue
Thorny hedgehogs, be not seen;
Newts and blind worms, do no wrong:
Come not near our fairy queen."

Barbie thought she was dreaming the voice. But can you be dreaming and cry at the same time? There were warm tears on her face, dripping saltily into her mouth.

Barbie sat up and pulled off the cloth that covered Emily's bird cage.

Mab was perched on the rung in the cage, swinging her bare legs.

"Mab!"

"Hush!" Mab said.

"You came back."

Mab examined her fingernails. "I'll leave again if you don't stop sniveling."

Barbie wiped her nose on her pajama sleeve. Tears fell into the cage, almost hitting Mab on the head.

"What's all this wet mess about?"

Barbie stared at the tear shining on the floor of the bird cage. For Mab it was almost the size of a puddle.

"You're right. I'm a klutz," Barbie said.

"I did not say klutz. I do not use words like klutz. Clumsy, perhaps."

"I don't care. I mean I hate ballet anyway and I don't want to be a model, but she got so mad!"

"She is vile."

"Don't say that."

"Vile vile vile. Like a crocodile."

"Stop."

Barbie had to admit that talking to Mab felt a lot like talking to herself sometimes; Mab said the things she would have liked to say.

"Well then, stop worrying about it. You can't help it if you're clumsy. I would be too if I had such big feet."

"Really?"

"No. But it's understandable."

Barbie looked down at her bare feet. They were tingling a little, the way they did in her dreams just before the Giant-thing happened. Hopefully she wouldn't start turning into a Giant.

She was glad when Mab said, "Let's get to work."

"On what?"

"Furnishings. I'll need proper furnishings for when I come to visit."

Barbie forgot about her Giant feet. She felt as light as Mab. "So you're going to stay with me!"

"The key word here is visit. V-I-S-I-T. I hope you know what *that* word means."

The sound of the toilet flushing made both Mab and Barbie jump. Barbie's senses had gotten more refined it seemed, since she'd known Mab—almost as if the rushing water might sweep her away into oblivion the way it could do to someone as little as the girl in the bird cage.

"I've got to go. See you later, alligator."

Barbie wondered if the alligator reference had something to do with the "vile vile like a crocodile" thing. She hoped Mab didn't think she, Barbie, was like her mother. But it was too late to ask. Mab was gone, out the open window.

"After a while, crocodile," Barbie said.

Actually, if anyone is a crocodile, Barbie thought, it's Hamilton Waverly. She was posing for him again, clutching a stuffed toy lion with matted orange fur. Hamilton Waverly's smile was long and toothy, sliding open under his nose.

"You said I could take your picture next time," said Barbie.

"How about if we set the timer and take one together," said Hamilton Waverly.

"I'd rather take one of you." Barbie wanted to be behind the Cyclops eye. She wanted to capture Mr. Crocodile. She could show the picture to Mab and they would laugh and draw devil horns and twirly-cue moustaches on it.

"Well, I'm flattered," said Hamilton Waverly. "But let's take one together first. Then next time, if you're very good, I'll teach you how to do it."

Barbie wished Mab was there. Mab would never have allowed this. But without Mab sometimes Barbie could hardly speak. She felt like the doll she had been named for, without even a hole where her mouth was supposed to be, as Hamilton Waverly came toward her.

When her mother knocked on the studio door, Barbie had never been so happy to hear her.

In between school, ballet, and photo sessions there was homework. And not just work for the classroom. Mrs. Marks had something else in mind for Barbie, besides math and English.

"Careful now. Stand up straight."

They were in the living room and Barbie was trying to balance one of her father's books of ancient mythology on her head. She would much rather have been reading it. Maybe she would absorb some of the information by osmosis through the cover.

After a while, when it seemed that all she was getting from the book on her head was a headache, she asked her mother if they could stop.

"Not until you really get it, Barbie. Believe me, you'll thank me for this when we get to the pageant."

"What?" The book slid off Barbie's head and thumped on the shag carpet.

"I only wish my mother had taken the time to do this with me when I was your age. I had to do everything myself. You have it much easier."

She picked up the book. "Oh, goodness! Can't you do anything right. Look!"

If Mab were here, Barbie thought, she would say, "What wouldn't stay on that stiff old bouffy wig of yours!" Or, "Maybe you just have a fat head . . . I mean *flat* head."

"Now try again," said Mrs. Marks. She put the book back on Barbie's head and off it slid.

"I give up. You'll have to practice on your own. The pageant is in three weeks."

"What pageant?"

But with a suddenness that almost reminded Barbie of Mab—well, not really, Mab never clunked, huffed, or jingled—Mrs. Marks was gone.

Barbie thought about the pageant thing for the rest of the afternoon. What was her mother talking about? There was no way Barbie could be in a beauty pageant. She would throw up or pass out with fear. She would trip on her dress and cry and then her mother would be even more furious than if she refused to participate at all. But to refuse seemed impossible. She sat down and picked up the book of mythology, opened it to an etching of a goddess springing from the brow of her father-god. Maybe Barbie's dad would help her.

At dinner that night Barbie picked carefully around the slab of veal on her plate. Once, she and Mab had discussed the human diet. Mab thought it was vile, uncouth, and evil to eat animals, especially baby ones. Maybe it was because she considered herself more like an animal than like a human, although far superior to your common lamb, of course.

"Barbie, eat your food," said Mrs. Marks,

who knew nothing of Mab's teachings, and would certainly not have listened to them even if she did.

"I can't," Barbie said.

"What do you mean you can't? It's not like balancing a book on your head. You just take your fork."

"And shove it," Mab would have said. Barbie just managed, "I don't eat slaughtered baby animals."

"You can't live on potatoes," said Mrs. Marks, dolloping more butter onto her mashed ones. "You'll get fat."

Barbie was surprised when her father looked up at this. He squinted through his glasses at Barbie's stick-figure arms.

"I don't think she has to worry about getting fat," he said.

Mrs. Marks sat up straighter as if she was trying to suck in her own gut. Barbie wondered if what her father had said had hurt her mother's feelings.

"It's never too early to start watching your weight. I wish someone had helped me with that before it was too late."

"Just let her eat what she wants," said Mr. Marks. "It's better that she eat her potatoes than nothing. She's getting too thin."

Barbie was glad he'd noticed. She thought it was the right time to let him know about her mother's plan. "Mom wants me to look good for the pageant," she said.

"What pageant?"

"The Model Child Pageant," said Mrs. Marks, glaring at Barbie. "All the little girls in it are on diets. They don't want to be jiggling up there on stage like middle-aged ladies."

Barbie was hoping that her father would protest, that he would insist that there would be no pageant, no diets, no baby animals. That he would take Barbie's hand and bring her to his office with him where he would read myths to her and she might be able to tell him about the Giants and even about Mab. But instead, without looking at his daughter, he asked, "What does she think about it?"

"She's a little nervous. But it'll be so much fun, won't it, Barbie."

Barbie just stared at her mother.

"Well, it isn't healthy," her father said, wearily removing his glasses and starting to wipe them with a corner of the white lace tablecloth until he remembered it was made of plastic.

"Oh and what is healthy? Your relationship with her? You never even say a word
to her."

Dr. Markowitz—it was still Markowitz
for him—got up and left the table.

"Just ignore him, honey," said Mrs. Marks.
You and I are going to have a lot of fun
preparing for this. You'll get to meet a lot of
other nice little girls. It'll be just like when we
played 'Supermodel' with your dolls, remember?" She reached over and patted Barbie's
head.

Barbie almost wished her mother had
gotten angry at her for telling her father about
the pageant. Then she would have more reason
to fight back. This way it was like they were
best friends planning slumber party games.

Barbie remembered playing "Supermodel"
with her mother. The dolls, Cindy, Claudia,
and Paulina, had seemed like they were
enjoying parading around in their lamé and
vinyl outfits. The thought of being one of
them hadn't seemed so bad then. Barbie's
mother never got angry when they played
"Supermodel." Her eyes became dream-clouds,
as if she were remembering her own career as
a heart-stopping sylph, swirling yards of silk

down runways where men with cameras,
all resembling Barbie's father as a young
intern, swooned to glimpse the legs beneath
her skirt.

Now the young doctor that Barbie's young
model mother had fallen in love with was a
beleaguered, balding man, whose headache
was getting worse by the moment as his wife
hollered at him. Barbie heard them through
the bedroom wall.

"How can you tell me how to raise my
daughter? You act like she doesn't even exist."

"It's impossible to discuss anything with
you," Barbie's father said, his voice constrict-
ing as if each word hurt him.

"Just leave then," said Barbie's mother.
Barbie turned off the flashlight, with which
she was looking at the girls with the Mabs in
their hands, and held her breath. "You're not
here anyway."

There was the sound of a door closing,
and heavy brown leather footsteps. Then the
sound of muffled percale pillowcase sobs.
Barbie peeked out from under her covers
as the front door closed—carefully, without

even the passion of a slam, which might have predicted its reopening sometime later on.

In the garden Mab was tightrope walking on a cobweb with a box of matches balanced on her head.

"How do you do that?" Barbie asked.

Mab kept taking tiny steps. The cobweb shivered and drops of dew pearled off onto the lower rose leaves. "Natural poise."

"I'm never going to be able to do it."

"Oh hush. Just try it and stop sniveling."

Barbie put the book with the pictures of the two girls and their winged friends onto her head, let go, and took a step. The book immediately slid off onto the wet grass and she dove to rescue it.

"See?" she said, dabbing at the damp cover with her nightgown.

"Well, you are hopeless. But I don't see why it matters if you can walk with a book on your head or not."

"My mom wants me to win this pageant thing."

"But you don't want to."

"Yes I do. For her." Barbie hated to hear

her mother cry. Since her father had left, the only time Mrs. Marks seemed happy was when they were planning the pageant.

"You just won't learn will you?" Mab said, tossing her head so that the matchbox dropped. "Okay, so pretend that it's not a book on your head. Pretend it's me. Or that little pigeon you used to have."

"Emily is a parakeet!" said Barbie. She was afraid she was going to start crying. Mab hated when she did that. It seemed like Mabs were unable to shed tears, at least as far as Barbie could tell.

Barbie closed her eyes, to squeeze away any telltale moisture, put the book on her head, opened her eyes, and began to walk, imagining Emily, the parakeet—not a pigeon at all—sitting prettily on a nest of her hair. The book stayed perfectly balanced. Barbie took it off her head and bowed to the rosebush audience.

"Wow! Thanks, Mab."

"Just don't forget to thank me in your acceptance speech."

Barbie leaned over to kiss her, but Mab whirred her wings like an engine and flew away. Kisses were almost as repellent to her as tears, Barbie figured. She picked up the balancing box of matches and tried to light one, but they were too damp.

Barbie wished she could have Mab around all the time. She probably could have helped with Barbie's klutziness, or clumsiness, in ballet class, for instance. That day Barbie stood in the back thinking of how well Mab moved. She tried to imitate the butterflyish gestures, rippling her back and letting her arms hover on the air. She didn't notice that Madame Molotov was staring at her through her bifocals until she heard the teacher's cane rap on the floor.

"What are you doing?"

Barbie stopped as dead as the ballerinas whose spirits she always imagined Madame Molotov was summoning.

"Why don't you share your little dance with the rest of the class, Miss Marko-*witz*." She emphasized the last syllable, spitting it out like a seed.

"No, thank you," Barbie said.

"Show us your combination," insisted the teacher through her stitched lips.

"Could I be excused, please?" asked Barbie, and it wasn't an excuse, she was suddenly in urgent need. "I have to use the bathroom."

"Not until you show us."

Her bladder swelling, sweat pouring from her pores, Barbie flapped her arms. The other girls giggled. Barbie shut her eyes. She imagined Mab there. She could see Mab perfectly—the breezy grassy ripple of her tiny spine, the blossomy toss of her hair, the wind-spun leaf-step of her feet. Soon she was dancing Mab. She didn't care what anyone thought. She was Mab; Mab was almost here, in her. The giggling stopped.

Then Madame Molotov rapped her cane again.

"That's enough!"

Barbie opened her eyes wide and realized where she was. Mab was not there, only Madame Molotov, the other students, their mothers, and Mrs. Marks, watching with the exasperated look of dead fish in a butcher shop.

In one of her father's books, Barbie had read about something called a Muse. The

Muse was the girl the poets invoked before they wrote their poem; she was the inspiration. Barbie wondered if maybe Mab was her muse. Not that she had done anything really artistic yet, but she would someday, she was sure—something better than her attempt at the dance in Madame Molotov's class. And no matter what it was, Mab would definitely be the inspiration for it, Barbie thought.

Now Mab was an inspiration to wake up in the morning, face the food at the dinner table, and keep a fake smile on—just knowing that later, maybe not that night but soon enough, she would appear winking with light and smiling a delicious poisonous smile.

Barbie wanted to give Mab something. She figured you should give your Muse gifts periodically, and besides, the bird cage hadn't been such a big hit. So she decided to furnish it. Using Popsicle sticks and cardboard she made tables and chairs. She sewed pillows and blankets out of scraps of material. Thimbles made good vases for tiny flowers. Matchboxes, stacked and glued together, made a chest of drawers.

One night, while she was working on the drawers, she heard the chirpy voice behind her, an arms-crossed-on-chest voice, a chin-stuck-out voice. "What's that supposed to be?"

Barbie turned and saw Mab with her arms crossed over her chest and her chin stuck out. She had flown through the open window and was hovering behind Barbie's shoulder, like a mosquito, Barbie thought, annoyed at Mab's tone. Although, what did she expect?

"It's a present for you," Barbie said. "You can put things in it."

Mab flew around in a circle, examining the piece of furniture. "Not much would fit."

"Most of your stuff is pretty small," said Barbie.

Mab sniffed at the chest of drawers.

"You hate it." Barbie threw it down and started crying. She couldn't do anything right. Even with the loveliest—if perhaps the cruelest—Muse around.

"Now stop that," Mab said.

Barbie kept crying. She wiped at her nose with her wrists, the way her mother hated. "I try so hard to be what she wants and I keep messing up."

"I told you," Mab said. "It doesn't matter what she wants."

"But I wanted to make some nice things

for you. And you hate everything. You're just like her."

For the first time, it seemed to Barbie, Mab stopped her constant humming, lit on Barbie's hand, and stayed very still, just watching. Barbie held her breath. In the usual blur of wings and color she hadn't ever really seen how Mab looked before.

Mab examined the chest of drawers. "It's a cute little piece, actually."

"Really?"

"It just needs handles."

Mab flew over to Barbie's fishbowl—empty of life since the death of Goldy and Sylvia Goldfish, but still a nice decoration, Barbie thought—and pointed through the glass at some tiny lacquered shells glinting in the sand. Barbie reached in and scooped them out. She held one up to a drawer of the chest that she had rescued from the carpet. Mab smiled like a pleased, although rather insatiable, interior decorator. Barbie could just imagine her scouting the stores on Beverly Drive for a Louis XIV chair, with her hair in a bun, pumps on her feet, followed by a trail of nervous salespeople.

Mab looked back in the fishbowl at the

miniature Empire State Building and Statue of Liberty. They were Barbie's favorite fishbowl decorations because they reminded her of the city where her father was from, and where she had always wanted to go. It seemed to her that she could become an artist there, like the people in books, who did not have pools or Astroturf or rosebushes or smog or houses the color and texture of lumpy guacamole, but had coffees and books on every corner and museums and theater and poetry readings in basements and streets where almost every shop sold wonderful black shoes with soles that were hard to wear out.

"And now, maybe you could get me that, too," Mab said, pointing at the statue of the stern girl with the star head, who probably had some cool black boots on under her robe.

After Barbie had fallen asleep on the floor, Mab sat in the bird cage examining her reflection in a makeup mirror Barbie had taken from her mother. She squeezed some juice from a flower in the thimble vase onto her finger and ran her finger over her lips, smacking them together like a mugging movie star.

Then she flew out of the bird cage, landed on Barbie's head, and kissed her cheek, leaving a tiny pink smudge.

Barbie never knew about the kiss but her dreams were different after it. Spun sugar clouds and extraterrestrial crystal vintage T-birds flying through space, morning-glory girls swinging from star-hung vines in cosmic gardens.

The kiss seemed to soothe Mab, too. She flew back into the bird cage, got into the Popsicle-stick bed, and closed her eyes.

Later, she heard a noise and flung herself under the bed. Mrs. Marks came in holding a large box. Mab trembled at the close call. If Barbie was afraid of the phantom Giants, it was nothing compared to Mab's fear of this real Giant who could assassinate her with just a whiff of its perfume.

"What are you doing?" Mrs. Marks shouted (to Mab it sounded like a shout).

Barbie opened her eyes and looked up at her mother. It seemed obvious what she was doing—sleeping on the floor, "until you came in," she wanted to say.

"Don't tell me you slept like that all night. You'll ruin your posture. And did you even wash your face?" She licked her thumb and bent to wipe away the flower lipstick smudge Mab had left, destroying the only clue to the fact that Barbie had been kissed.

From beneath the Popsicle-stick bed Mab eyed the open window, measuring her chances for escape.

"I brought you something," Mrs. Marks said, putting down the box.

It must be some beauty products or a new dress for the pageant, Barbie thought. Mrs. Marks went over and closed the window. The sound made Mab jump, hitting her head on a Popsicle stick.

"Don't you know what day it is?"

Barbie shook her head. She was thinking about Mab and how she never allowed closed windows when she was inside the house.

"You really are too much."

Oh no, Barbie thought. The pageant?

"It's your birthday," said her mother.

Barbie sat up, relieved. She knew she had to get her mother out of there so she could open the window for Mab. "I'm kind of hot," she said, looking at the window.

"It's freezing in here. You're shivering. What are you talking about? Open your gift."

Barbie ripped the Barbie doll paper off the package. Inside was a deluxe beauty-queen doll with a bouquet of roses and a ribbon across her chest reading MISS BEAUTIFUL.

"Thanks, Mom," Barbie said.

Mab could not help making a choking sound. It was too faint to really hear, but somehow it caused Mrs. Marks to turn and see the bird cage. Barbie's heart contracted like an animal that has misbehaved and is awaiting punishment. Luckily Mab had disappeared farther under the bed. But Mrs. Marks wasn't looking for Mabs. She was concerned about a bird cage that had been missing for quite some time now. Not to mention a missing parakeet, although that was less of an issue really. The bird had been a bit of a pest.

"You took this? Why would you do that? Where's that bird?"

"I let Emily go."

"Honestly, Barbie," said Mrs. Marks. "You have everything any little girl could possibly want and you go around stealing bird cages."

"I'm sorry, Mom."

"I don't know why I continue to buy you things. You don't appreciate anything." She had the tearful sound in her voice again. That was what got Barbie. The anger never worked as well as that.

Mrs. Marks went over to the bird cage. Barbie jumped up, ready to tackle her mother down if necessary, teary voice and all, for Mab's sake, but Mrs. Marks flung up her arms, sighed, and walked out.

Mab darted out from under the bed and flew to the window, beating her wings against it in a manic frenzy. Barbie was afraid the wings would crumble to dust against the glass.

"Let me out!" Mab wailed, if something that tiny could be called a wail.

"She didn't see you."

"She could have." Mab shuddered. "Vile! Vile!" Shreds of wing flew into the air.

"Stop it!" Barbie said. "You'll hurt yourself. Calm down and I'll open it."

Mab stopped beating and looked over at the doll Barbie's mother had brought. "And speaking of vile. What's that thing?"

"She's almost as pretty as you are," Barbie said, hoping this would make Mab stay a little longer.

It worked. Mab flew over to the doll. "Ack! She is not."

"I said almost."

"Her titties are weird-looking. And look at her feet. Why are they like that?"

"So she can wear high heels." Barbie had to admit, she had wondered the same thing the first time she got one of the dolls. But now she was used to the precarious teetering slant of the plastic feet. "My mom gets me one every year."

She dragged a box full of Barbies and a couple of Kens out from under the bed and grabbed two bouquets of them by the feet. Then she put them down and held the new beauty-queen doll up next to her reflection in the mirror.

"She named me after her. She wishes I looked like this."

"What? Like a plastic thing with weird feet and pointed boobs?"

Barbie and Mab giggled. Then Barbie stopped and looked down at her flat chest. She didn't really care whether or not she looked like her namesake. But if she did look like her, maybe her mother would be happier. Maybe she'd win the pageant and her father would be proud and come back to them. It seemed as if creatures with weird feet and big pointed boobs were never sorrowful.

＊

At one time Sis Los Angeles had carried a Mab around in her pocket like Teeny did. The Mab whispered to her about how it had once been—orchards of fruit trees instead of freeways, skies so clear you could hear the stars singing, flowers growing over every house, deer and coyotes racing through the backyards, the ocean visible from every hilltop, swirling with mermaids and sea dragons of foam. Sis loved these stories; they made her feel better when she was lonely. The Mab sang them to her like lullabies.

That was when she was different too. She never wore makeup or shoes. She ran around stealing avocados off the neighbors' trees and poaching roses from their gardens. Being touched was not a terrifying thing, then, although she couldn't sit still long enough to tolerate much of it.

Then one day, something happened. The Mab in her pocket was taken away from her. Sis appeared the next day in an ad where she wore lipstick. She looked ten years older than she was. Pedophilic feelings were aroused in non-pedophiles on line at the market. The Mab was not strong enough to stay around and help. Mabless Sis grew stranger and stranger. She had more and more operations as she grew older—operations to shrink her nose until it was almost invisible, operations to increase the size of her breasts until they seemed to be toppling off the billboards on which she lay, reigning over the city. In restaurants she insisted on special lighting. She combed her hair with a plastic doll comb and dressed her cat in doll dresses. When the little girl who looked a lot like she had once looked was found murdered, she collected all the tabloids and papered her bathroom walls with the face of a tiny dead beauty queen. Sometimes at night, she thought she heard a child's sobs dripping out of the faucet.

When Barbie ran out of the studio that day, she remembered one thing in particular. It was the face of the boy who was being dragged into the building by his pretty young mother. The boy and his mother had hair like sunlight falling through branches and alien-blue eyes. But what struck Barbie most about the boy was the expression on his face. She knew it was a mirror of her own.

She wanted to stop the boy from going into Hamilton Waverly's studio. But he had already disappeared through the door.

Mrs. Marks found her daughter running down the sidewalk past a man crouched over a sign asking for change. The man had dirt-encrusted bare feet and was missing his front teeth. Mrs. Marks was less concerned with the bloodless pallor of her daughter's face and the fact that she was running from Hamilton Waverly's studio than with the idea that Barbie was on the streets with the bums. At least, that was something that was easier to be consciously upset about.

"There you are!" she shouted, slamming to a stop alongside her ghosty-white child. "You scared me to death. Why didn't you wait for me?"

Barbie just stared at her.

"Get in the car. What's wrong with you?"

Barbie felt the tears and tried to swallow

them, but the salty lump burst. Mrs. Marks got out and went around the car. When she patted her daughter's back, Barbie flinched. The patting made it seem like she was being comforted for dropping her ice-cream cone on the sidewalk.

"Don't cry," Mrs. Marks said. "Life is full of problems." She stopped, remembering something and then waved her hand in the air as if brushing away an invisible insect. "I've had my share too, believe me. You just have to learn to deal with them."

The way she dealt with this one was to stop at a fast-food drive-thru for two hot dogs. The dog might have helped her feel less empty and light-headed, but it didn't help Barbie, who tossed hers out the window.

Mab, like Barbie, dreamed of New York. She figured that there, her beauty might be recognized. Barbie had told her that according to what her father used to say, people accepted and even appreciated eccentricities more there. Not that Mab considered herself an eccentricity, but she was certainly smaller than the normal standard of beauty. And her wings were unusual in the San Fernando Valley. She and Barbie had looked through an *Interview* magazine where men from Manhattan wore ugly, gaudy gauze attempts at Mab's wings and pranced around. At least they were taking a stab at loveliness, Mab thought, as she flew in circles above the Empire State Building that Barbie had brought out into the garden for her. Better than here.

Mab was trying to take her mind off Barbie, who was sitting at the side of the pool weeping and tearing up photographs of herself. Mab did not want to ask her why she was crying—she really didn't want to know. She wished they could just get to New York, somehow, and forget all this business.

Finally she said, "You cry more than anyone I've ever met, Pigeon."

Mab hoped that the name might make Barbie mad enough to stop crying, but it didn't work. Barbie kept on. She lit a match and held it up to a picture of her face.

Mab, imagining singed wings, whirred backward. "Be careful with that!" Suddenly she was really annoyed. Here was Barbie, with the opportunity for fame, fortune, and endless attention at her young fingertips, weeping and lighting photos on fire in a way that could endanger gossamer beyond repair. "You really don't have it so bad," she said, "if you think about it. I mean, you get to have your picture taken all the time. You're going to be a star."

Barbie began to sob and threw the flaming picture into the pool.

The sight of fire had made Mab's eyes blaze. "I wish I could be famous. No one ever gets to see me except you. I wish someone would take *my* picture once in a while."

Barbie lit another match. Mab braved its heat and used all the breath in the waify wraith of her body to blow it out. She hardly had any left to say, "Stop that! What is wrong with you?"

"'Just learn to deal with your problems.' It was like she knew. And she wasn't going to do anything."

Barbie held up a picture of herself and Hamilton Waverly. Mab felt queasy looking at it. He was like some slimy liver-breathed kind of thing that should have stayed under its rock.

Suddenly Mab understood. She really should have known before, she told herself. She should have seen it coming. But as sophisticated as she was in the world of ladybugs and butterflies and crickets—a diva, a princess, an ambassadrix of cool—she still hadn't really learned that much about the Big World, even with all the *Vogue* and *Vanity Fair* and *New York Times* articles Barbie got for her to read. It was really an uglier place than she would have liked to believe. It had no respect for its smallest and most delicate members. It would let them starve like the children in the back pages with pot bellies and empty-soup-pot eyes; it would let them be touched in ways that no one should be touched, and broken like wishbones and tossed in the trash.

Mab reached for a match. Barbie held the matchbox steady and Mab struck. The flame was brighter and redder than Mab's hair. Mab touched it to the corner of the photograph.

The photo began to curl in on itself as the fire ate. Barbie tossed the burning picture into the pool. She and Mab watched it blaze like a firefish in the blue water.

PART II

I Was a Teenage Fairy

Imagine the blazing
pool dissolving into the flame of a match
lighting a cigarette. You know by the
sight of the girl smoking the cigarette that
five years have passed. She is sixteen. Her
beauty, which before she might have
doubted, should be undeniable now, but
she feels even less beautiful after the
thing that happened when she was
eleven. She wears heavy eye makeup like
an Egyptian mummy and her body is very
thin. She believed that being thin might
get them to leave her alone, but actually
the reverse was true, it made them lavish
more praises upon her. And she doesn't
have the choice to ward them off with
weight—first of all she can't gain, no matter how much she eats, and also, it would

make her too much like the Giants whom she dreams about even more often now.

Even though she is past the age of imaginary friends, the friend she might sometimes think is imaginary is still with her. The friend has not aged at all; maybe their life spans are different, maybe she is just so small that no one would notice her aging, maybe she is just too vain to allow for wrinkles. She is walking along the girl's arm, balancing a box of cigarettes on her head.

"I wish you could go with me tonight," Barbie said to Mab.

"*You* wish? I'm the one who's stuck here with the ladybugs."

"I could put you in my purse."

"Oh please, what do you think I am? An eye pencil?"

"Well then, you could just fly around next to me."

"In a perfect world! I'm not going to risk getting squashed to death by some vile drunken imbecile."

"I'll protect you."

Mab rolled her eyes. "I hate to remind you of this but you can't even protect yourself very well."

Barbie knew Mab was right. It didn't exactly make her feel great, though. "So I guess you'll have to stay home again," she said.

Mab smacked her lips. "Just make sure you give me a play-by-play account of the action."

Barbie nodded, but she knew she'd probably disappoint Mab again. Mab always wanted to hear about how Barbie had had some hot sex, and there was never anything to tell.

"Let me know if there are any biscuits. And do *everything* I would do," said Mab.

Barbie stood at the bottom of the canyon where the cars rushed by, sending tremors through the oleander bushes. She was chomping on her gum so hard that her jaw ached. Hitch-hiking was stupid, she knew, but she did it anyway. As if she were invincible. Besides, what could hurt her anymore, really? It would hurt worse to stay at home with the crocodile, remembering. This way she could feel the rush of warm air, blowing back her hair as if she were a plant. She could go out into the night and become a part of it and forget who she was.

When the man stopped, she hesitated. Usually she tried to hitch only with women. But she'd been waiting a long time and she wanted to get to the party. The night was starting to cool down.

Plus, he was an older guy, pretty respectable-looking.

But of course, as soon as she got in, he was taking bites out of her with his eyes.

"You are stunning. Truly. You must be a model."

Barbie wondered how they could tell these things with all the big clothes she always wore. It was like they had some sixth sense or something. She shrugged.

"Mind if I smoke?" she asked.

The man pulled out the ashtray. "Go ahead." He was staring at her chest as if her breasts were exposed. He'd be disappointed if he saw how small they are, Barbie thought, but it didn't stop him from gaping.

"Do you have a boyfriend?"

Barbie took a deep drag on her cigarette. "Yeah."

"He's a lucky man," letched the driver.

"Thank you," Barbie said sweetly. Her fingers gripped the cigarette so hard that they started to cramp.

"What's he like?" There was something nauseating about the man's tone. Like he would get off later on some vision of her and Boyfriend having sex.

Barbie put on her best psycho tone, widening her eyes to manic proportions and contorting her mouth. "He's this Giant. And he carries this huge weapon around his neck. He uses it to cut out your soul and then he keeps it in there. So you can never get away from him."

It had worked. The man flinched. Barbie blew smoke out the window into the cloud-smoked night.

The former hotel that Todd Range now owned and lived in was infamous, in the trendiest, and therefore most positive sense of the word. The young Hollywood scenesters frequented it on weekends in their vintage cars and on their Harleys, wearing their black-leather platform motorcycle boots and lavish tattoos and seeking out titillating new drugs to crack the jade casings that had formed around their senses. It was a large old building on one of the north-south streets that swept up toward the Hollywood sign and down toward the freeways, decorated with stone friezes depicting weapon-winged angels and fork-tongued gargoyles. When Todd Range decided he wanted to party, he would park his cherry-pink-and-black 1950s Lincoln Continental at the front curb. It was like a flag. As soon as it appeared, the hipsters and hipstrixes started arriving in droves, loping or skulking up the stone stairs to the beat of the music gyrating from within.

When Barbie got there the party was already raving. It reminded her of some kind of mythological creature trancing out in an ecstatic dance. A Giant, but a very beautiful one—a hermaphrodite belly dancer with the cheekbones of a wild cat. Barbie smiled at the picture in her head. She would have liked to tell Mab about it.

As she walked inside, an androgynous-looking boy with very short soft hair stared at her. Barbie stared back. There was something familiar about him that she couldn't place. He was probably in some band she'd seen, or in some commercial, maybe.

Barbie walked down a hallway full of wrought-iron sconces holding burning candles, and decorated with medieval-looking leather-and-iron furniture. A boy was chasing a girl around a suit of armor that looked as if it were about to reach out and swat them in the head with its silver hand.

Some shallow steps led down into a courtyard where the mosaic fountain was spurting jets of blood-red wine. People were filling glasses or tilting their heads back and sucking it straight into their mouths.

Barbie was heading for the wine when a girl came up to her.

"Aren't you Barbie Marks? I'm Ashley Wells."

Barbie looked blank.

"I was in the Model Girl Pageant with you?" Ashley said, stressing the question mark at the end as if to emphasize Barbie's poor memory.

"Oh. Yeah. Sure. Hi." Barbie didn't want to be rude but she didn't really remember much about the pageant at all.

"It looks like you've got quite the *phat* career going on," Ashley said.

Barbie shrugged.

"I saw you in *Sis-Girl* last month."

"Are you still modeling?" Barbie asked, to take the focus off. She was sure Ashley had plenty to say about her own career.

"Oh, no. I am so over that *wack* stage of the life. I've been actin' up."

Barbie just looked at her.

"You know—*acting*?"

"Sure," Barbie said. Actin' up. Whatever. "That's cool."

"I just did a movie about teen modeling with Todd and Griffin Tyler. It's the *bomb*."

"Cool," Barbie said.

Ashley came closer, staring at Barbie's hair and face as if she were trying to find split ends or, better yet, a pimple. "So how do you know Todd?"

Barbie was starting to get it. "I don't really. We met at a party last week."

Having not found split ends or pimples (Mrs. Marks never allowed them) but having decided that Barbie was too thin—a little on the anorexic side, even—and weird-looking and probably smoked and drank too much, Ashley had backed off a little. "Oh really? He didn't tell me. You think he'd tell me that he met such a famous model."

That was when Todd Range came over. Todd Grunge, Barbie thought. He had the required goatee, scraggly hair, and grubby clothes. But even the grunge-wear could not dull the brilliant polished-mineral black of his eyes or lessen the effect of his lavish eyelashes, pouting lips, or leanly muscled babe-of-life body. A biscuit, as Mab would say.

"Hey." He looked into Barbie's eyes as if there wasn't anyone else in the room.

She smiled at him, dizzily.

Ashley looked at Todd, then Barbie, then Todd. She was pissed.

"Todd, Barbie and I know each other from when we were kids," she said.

"Cool. Did you work together?"

"We were in this stupid pageant thing," Barbie said.

"Barbie won."

There was a hefty silence. Barbie's skin tickled as if Mab were running up and down her body. She wished Mab *was* there.

"So Barbie, can I get you a drink?"

She could really use one, even though she wasn't sure how many she'd need to ward off the Uzis of anger coming out of Ashley's eyes at her. "Thanks."

He went to fill a glass from the fountain. Ashley already had a mineral water—which was all she ever drank—but that didn't make her any less angry that Todd hadn't asked her if she wanted something too.

"I hope you know I'm not going to be your runner-up anymore, girlfriend. You might have been cuter when we were little, but your tits never lived up to your namesake."

"Fuck off, bitch."

"What did you say?" Ashley looked like she was going to dig her fingernails into Barbie's eyes, which were even wider than usual after hearing the voice and wondering if schizophrenia was setting in, or if Mab was really there. Or if there was a difference between the two possibilities.

"Nothing!" Barbie said.

"You watch it, Miss *Thing*."

Ashley thrust her hands around in some kind of attempt at a gang gesture and walked away. Barbie opened her tiny lime-green vinyl purse and looked inside. Guess who was looking up at her with eyes even greener and shinier than the vinyl?

"What the . . ." Barbie started to say.

"You didn't think I was going to stay

home again while you go out and have fun every night, did you?" said Mab.

"You shouldn't have said that to her. She already hates me."

"*She's* hateful!" Mab ducked back inside the purse. "Watch out, here comes the biscuit."

Todd handed Barbie her drink with that same you-and-me-alone-on-a-desert-island look in his pirate eyes. She smiled and looked away.

"This is a great place."

"I think it's pretty cool. It must have been wild when it was an operating hotel."

"How did you find it?"

"They're using it as a set in the next thing I'm doing."

Barbie looked up at the glass skylights above the courtyard. They were painted with a night sky, dark violet blue and starred, the way she had read skies are supposed to look.

"Do you want to see some of the upstairs?"

She followed him up the staircase decorated with carved and real nymphs in various stages of undress. The candlelit rooms were furnished with overstuffed worn satin couches and potted palms. Faded medieval-style tapestries covered the walls.

"It would be an amazing place to shoot," Barbie said.

"You could use it if you want."

She realized he thought she meant she wanted her picture taken here. But what she wanted was to photograph him, shadows from the candelabra hollowing out his cheekbones even deeper, Mab flitting behind him like his thoughts.

"I'd like to take your picture."

"Are you a photographer too?"

"I wish. I always wanted to be."

He lowered his head and lifted his arms in the air, waving his hands like a mad Houdini. "This is the magic hotel. Ask and you shall receive. Seek and you shall find."

He gestured for her to follow him into the next room. The only furniture in it was a giant bed with carved wooden posts thicker around than Barbie and twice as tall. There was also a wooden cabinet with Adam and Eve carved on its panels. One of the knobs was the apple in Eve's hands. Todd pulled it and the cabinet opened. It was filled with cameras. He chose one and gave it to Barbie.

"What's this for?" She was suspicious. But it wasn't like he could have thought he had to give it to her to get her to sleep with him. If he wanted that, he probably figured he could just smile the right way and offer her another glass of wine, right?

"Consider it a favor to me," Todd said. "I like to think of myself as a kind of patron of the arts. It feeds my ego to be able to give it to you."

Oh, so that was it. Control freak. It figures, Barbie thought. If his eyes didn't twinkle so much, like he was laughing at himself, he'd never get away with it. But she said, "I don't think you need that to make you feel good about yourself. Every one I know is in love with you."

He frowned and shook his head. "They love an image." Looked into her eyes again. She realized that that look of his—it wasn't just about him pretending they were alone somewhere, away from the world, Garden of Eden style—it made *her* feel that way. "You probably know something about that?"

She'd forgotten what he was talking about. Oh—everyone being in love with an image of you. She didn't, really. Her mother kept her so sheltered. But she knew boys had her picture up over their beds to look at when they jerked off. So maybe she understood.

"Todd?" It was Ashley. She came into the room with a look on her face that reminded Barbie of the serpent on the cabinet. A forked tongue might slither out at any second. "Todd, come down stairs, honey. Cheyenne and Reggie are here."

The white home-girl ebonics had vanished now. She was playing the princess of the palace. She reached for Todd's hand and pulled him to the door.

Mab peeked out of Barbie's purse and watched Todd's butt walk away.

"Mmmm-mmmm. Biscuit," she smacked.

"He's too big for you," Barbie said.

"Oh really! You've learned quite a lot about him."

"Ha ha."

Another door opened, and the boy Barbie had seen when she first arrived, the one with the exquisite face, came into the room. Mab hid back in the bag.

"Oh, sorry," Boy said. He was nervous, maybe strung out. "Have you seen Todd?"

"He went downstairs with Ashley."

The boy brushed a long lock of sun-streaked brown hair out of his slanted blue eyes. "You look real familiar to me," he said.

"You too," said Barbie. She felt like she had to talk very softly so he wouldn't run off, like a frightened blue-eyed deer.

"I mean, not from pictures or whatever. Like didn't we meet one time?"

"Maybe a long time ago."

"Was it on that jeans ad or something?"

Barbie shook her head, looking at him. Then suddenly she thought she remembered. "I don't think so. I think it was . . ."

She paused, not really wanting to say. And he didn't want her to, she could tell by the fear in his eyes that were suddenly wide open without the camouflage of the long thick lashes. He was the boy at Waverly's studio, the one she had wanted to warn. "I'm Griffin," he said quickly, so she couldn't remind him.

"Barbie Marks."

When he smiled he looked even younger. But then he seemed nervous again.

"Well. I better go find Todd. See ya."

"'Bye." Barbie, and Mab, who had popped up again, watched him leave.

"Now that one isn't even a biscuit! He's . . . maybe a croissant. An eclair. Mmmm."

"Mab, you are so bad."

"You'd get horny too if all you ever got to look at were grasshoppers and ants and toads. Not even horny toads."

"Well, he is a babe."

"But I bet he's a biscuit-lover."

"I don't think so. Androgyny's trendy."

"Trust me. I have perfect instincts for this. And that other one might dabble too."

This implication about Todd annoyed Barbie more than she wanted to admit. "You say that about everyone."

"Only about everyone interesting!" Mab was suddenly aware of Barbie's camera. That, combined with the delicious thought of everyone interesting and their controversial sexual preferences, had excited her to near-mania. "Take my picture!" she squealed, flying out of the bag and shimmering seductively in the air like a perfectly lit 1940s glamour-queen movie star.

Barbie held up the camera to shoot. But before she had succeeded, a band of giggling party-goers stumbled into the room and Mab, her fantasies of immortalized grandeur shattered—temporarily—flew back into the vinyl purse.

Mrs. Marks had dropped Barbie off at
the agency while she did some shopping in
Beverly Hills. They were going to meet at the
deli for lunch. Barbie was on her way there,
imagining the fight over not eating smoked
fish on her bagel, when she saw a man walking down the street.

She turned and followed him for a couple
of blocks, sure, but not letting herself be, until
he stopped at a red light and she caught up
with him and saw the side of his face, close
enough to touch.

"Dad?"

He turned around and looked at her coldly.

"Hi, Dad."

"Hello."

He seemed younger, somehow; he wasn't
wearing a tie.

"How are you?" Barbie asked.

"I'm well, thank you, and you?" It sounded
as if he were talking to a client.

The light changed. He hesitated. It seemed
as if he were about to reach out and touch
her shoulder. But instead he looked away.
"Well. It was nice seeing you. Take care." And

Dr. Markowitz stepped off the curb.

He was hurrying home to his new family. His daughter, Rebecca, who was so different from Barbie. Dr. Markowitz watched over her like a Papa Bear. He held her hand so tight it hurt as he walked her to the private school with the big gates. She would not be allowed to wear makeup until she was much much older. The danger of cigarette smoke was a common topic at the dinner table. But Rebecca would not grow up to feel angry about these things. Every morning at breakfast her father asked her if she wanted to share her dreams with him; he never forced it but she liked to tell him sometimes. He read her Greek myths as bedtime stories. They told each other funny animal jokes—the same ones again and again. Rebecca looked just like her mother, with big brown eyes and long brown-velvet curls. They wrote and illustrated little storybooks together, made matzoh ball soup, took the dogs to the park every day, did a mother-daughter yoga class.

Rebecca had no need for a Mab.

Barbie stayed on the corner biting the inside of her lip until she thought it might bleed. She imagined blood on her white T-shirt and how the Beverly Hills shoppers would all pretend they didn't notice or assume that she'd undergone some plastic surgery.

"Vile!" Mab said.

She was on the garden table inside the deluxe doll house that Barbie had received for her twelfth birthday and that they had both hated until they decided it was just tacky enough to make a perfect kitsch hotel and spa. Now Mab was stretched out on the floor doing leg lifts.

"I can't believe how cold he was," Barbie said.

"Forget about it," said Mab, flipping onto her back for a set of sit-ups. "He's just vile."

"He is obviously so ashamed of me."

Mab frowned and Barbie braced, knowing she was going into her analytical mode.

"He was probably turned on by you on some level and couldn't handle the Oedipal, or rather, Electric, repercussions."

"Gross! I am so sick of your sex-based theories. And it's Electra, not Electric."

"Electral. But I think Electric sounds better. You should really let me analyze you,

Pigeon. If someone like him could be a shrink wrap, I could do it. My Goddess, that man has less perception than a . . ." She pushed Ken, who was lying on the floor near her, and he fell out of the house and off the wrought iron garden table.

Barbie picked him up and looked at him.

"I don't know why I let him stay in here," Mab said.

"I do," said Barbie.

"Well, he is much better than those females. But not much. Look at that crotch!"

Barbie laughed in spite herself. For something so little, Mab had the sex drive of a family of large rabbits.

I might have been like that, too, she thought, if things had been different.

"I once knew someone who should have a crotch like that. So he couldn't do any more damage."

Mab tapped her finger against her lips and nodded thoughtfully. If she owned a pair of miniature spectacles she would have put them on at this point.

"The doctor is *in*," she said.

Once Mab decided it was time for analysis it was pretty hard to get her to give it up. She was like a bird sucking a worm out of the ground, Barbie thought.

She was lying on her bed with Mab perched near her head, scribbling things down on a matchbook. Barbie figured she'd try to oblige and get it over with. Besides, she thought, what if it helps? Mab had been the only source of comfort in her whole life, even if sometimes she didn't seem to know what she was talking about.

"Maybe I let that man do those things to me because my father never gave me enough attention."

"Hmmm. Interesting theory. You're starting to sound like me. But it's not valid. You're just taking the blame on yourself to avoid confronting the full-scale victimization you underwent."

"I don't think this analysis is helping much," Barbie said.

"Of course you don't. You're resisting change. You want to stay locked in your self-preserving neuroses." Mab had been reading *Psychology Today*.

Barbie wanted to swat her like a mosquito. Self-preserving neuroses! What about Mab's neuroses! Mab's whole self was a neurosis, actually. "I can't believe I listen to a stupid . . ."

Mab's wings curled up with fury, but her voice didn't change and she was still hiding out behind Barbie on the pillow. "A what?"

"Nothing," Barbie mumbled.

"What were you going to call me? Say it. It will help me understand you better."

"Insect," Barbie said. "I called you an insect. You hurt my . . ."

"What did you call me?" the wing-curling fury was in her voice now.

Barbie turned to look at her but she flew into the air. "You've called me names for years, Mab. You said I was a pigeon with a bulbous head and klutzy feet."

"You are. A pigeon with an enormous bulbous empty head that cannot even remember that I do not, under any circumstances, use the word klutzy. And I'm not going to waste my time looking into that vast abyss anymore. You don't even pay me!"

She spat the juice from the flower she had been sucking at Barbie and flew out the window.

The juice had just missed Barbie's eye. She wiped it from her cheek. She was glad Mab was gone or she might have squashed her.

"Pay you?" she screamed out the window. "I give you houses and cars and Statues of Liberties ... Liberty .. ."

Of course, Mab probably didn't hear. But the neighbors get another show, Barbie thought, wondering if one day someone would tell her mother about her conversations with an invisible friend, and she'd be locked up.

Barbie threw herself down onto the mattress in a state of post-therapy exhaustion. She thought about the fact that therapists are called shrinks and how appropriate that was for hers.

The phone rang. Barbie almost let the machine get it, but then she changed her mind and pounced. Maybe it would miraculously be a real friend, for once, to take her away from this obsessive relationship she and Mab had.

It was Todd Range. His voice was husky, sort of rough and sparkling at the same time— Barbie imagined unpolished diamonds. She was so entranced with the sound of it that it took her a while to realize that he was asking her out, and for her to agree.

When she hung up she jumped off the bed and stared at her reflection with eyes that she still thought were too big and round, a little like a cartoon character's. And I'm built like Tweetie too, she thought, pushing up her small breasts with her hands. But if anyone could give her back her desire, it was Todd Range.

Todd took Barbie to The Slammer, a punk nightclub in Hollywood, so hot, small and close that your clothes and hair soaked up the smoke in five minutes and you could taste beer in your mouth when you walked through the door. He got her in effortlessly, even though she was too young to drink, and escorted her to a VIP booth by the stage where Wig Starbuck, punk grandpa of the scene, was playing for the moshing youngsters.

"It's so cool that you know him!" Barbie shouted into Todd's ear as Wig flexed his sinewy, ornately tattooed arms and crooned like a hard-core Sinatra.

Todd grinned. "He's a really cool guy. I hope I'm doing shit like this when I'm a fogey."

"You will. You'll never be a fogey." She ran her hands over her bare shoulders as she watched Wig thrash around. "I want some tattoos like that."

Todd looked at her out of the corner of his eye and said sternly, "No you don't."

"You sound like the crocodile."

"Who?"

Sometimes she forgot that she wasn't talking to Mab, who shared her language. But being with Todd was worth having to explain. Mab would have been a drag at a club, complaining about the smoke or the possibility of being squashed by a steel-toed boot. And she wouldn't have looked half as good with a scruffy patch of hair growing on her chin. Come to think of it, who would? Todd was ridiculously biscuit. "My mother."

"It's just that you might change your mind about them later."

"Not if I'm a cool oldster like him," Barbie said. Now Wig was dancing with a zebra-headed chick who had joined him on the stage. She seemed to like his tattoos, too. And she had plenty of her own but they looked kind of like the homemade-while-under-the-influence type.

"Do you have any?" Barbie asked Todd. She couldn't see them on his bare biceps, but there was a lot more of that body under the black T-shirt and Levi's.

Todd looked uncomfortable, like a Mab had crawled inside his T-shirt. "Not really," he said.

"Not *really?*"

He cleared his throat and took a swig of beer. Barbie watched a vein in his neck twitch. He wiped his lips with the back of his hand and squinted at her. "So, tell me something about you."

"I did. I told you that I wanted a tattoo." She tapped his vein-laced wrist with her fingernail. "Now you're supposed to show me yours."

Wig Starbuck was finishing the set, down on his knees with his sweaty tattoos shining. Todd got up and took Barbie's hand.

"Let's get backstage before the masses," he said.

She wondered what misshapen bong or other embarrassment was drawn on him.

Maybe it was to get Todd back a little for being so mysterious that Barbie let Wig Starbuck, Punk Grandpa, sign his name on her T-shirt. He was a gentleman about it, and avoided her breasts, but he did seem to be enjoying the whole experience. This would have bothered Barbie if it were anyone else but Wig. She had albums of his that were twice as old as she was and that she used to kiss before she went to bed at night when she was thirteen. She wondered how he had survived all this time; his tattoos were woven around track marks and scars from where he used to cut himself on stage.

"I love your tattoos," Barbie told him.

He still had the gorgeous lamplike smile that was captured on the cover of his first album, *Eat Your World*, and that Barbie had kissed so often as a child. His sinewy, perfect body looked smaller close up. And he spoke like a real gentleman, in a soft voice that surprised her. "Thank you. I'm sure I'd love yours too."

"I don't have any yet," Barbie told him. She frowned at Todd. "He says I shouldn't get any."

"*He* should get one," Wig Starbuck said, kissing her hand. "Of your name inside a heart."

She looked over at Todd who was sucking on a cigarette. She couldn't tell if he was still upset about the tattoo thing or if he was a little jealous of Wig. Either way, she knew he wanted to leave.

When they got back to Todd's, they found Griffin in front of the fireplace with its ornate carvings of masklike faces. Todd brought out a bottle of wine and they joined him on the wine-red carpet with its thick pattern of roses and pomegranates.

Griffin didn't say much; he was staring at the shower of firework embers behind the grate and smoking a joint. Barbie wondered if he'd rather be alone, but it seemed like Todd wanted him there.

"You know, you two kind of look alike," Todd said. "Maybe it's your eyes. Not just the color. They're really sad."

"Mine look that way because of the dark circles from smoking so much," said Barbie.

"They're beautiful. The sadness makes you even more beautiful."

Griffin, who was lying on his stomach, flipped over on his back and stared up at the beamed ceiling.

"How'd you start modeling?" Todd asked Barbie.

"My crazy mother. She used to do it and she never made it the way she wanted."

"See, I told you you and Griffin are the same. That's what happened to him."

"What about you?"

"My parents were these hippie artist types and they encouraged us all to do what we were into."

"You're lucky," Barbie said.

"Sort of. But I think they gave me a little too much freedom."

"What's that?"

Todd poured more wine and handed her the glass, letting his fingers linger on the stem before he let go. The fire winked in his eyes. "What would you do if you could do anything?"

She felt a funny tossing feeling low down in her stomach and she wanted it to stop; she knew it was just what he had intended for her to feel. "I don't know. Go to New York. Do something creative."

He leaned closer as if he were going to touch her wrist. "Have you used your camera yet?"

When she didn't answer, he said, "You'll probably be great. You've been on the other side of it for so long that you'll really get how it feels."

"I don't feel much anymore when someone takes my picture."

"You sound like Griffin," Todd said. "What are you guys, secret siblings?" He paused and swallowed the last drops of wine in his glass. She watched the movement of his throat. "But I'll tell you, when people see those pictures they feel something."

Barbie shrugged, took a big hit of the joint and handed it to Griffin, who was sitting up now, cross-legged, watching Todd. He took a hit, handed it back.

"I'm going up. See ya."

They said good night and Barbie watched him climb the stairs. She looked away too soon to see Mab fly out of her purse and follow him.

Barbie had been a little uneasy with Griffin there, but now the thought of being alone with Todd felt even stranger. She wished she could tell him something about herself that would ease the fear in her. If he knew what had happened it might make him go more slowly.

"You know, Griffin and I saw each other

before. When we were kids," she said.

"On a shoot?"

She nodded.

"He's an incredible guy. He gets really bummed out a lot though. I thought it might help him to work on that film we did."

"Have you always taken care of everybody?" Barbie asked.

"Only the people I care about. And unfortunately they all need it. The world can treat you like shit if you're at all sensitive."

Barbie realized her arms were crossed tight over her chest. She let them drop and felt the heat from the fire pour its glow to her breasts.

"Do you ever let anyone take care of you?" she asked him. Suddenly it wasn't so important to tell him about herself. She wanted him to tell her something. She wanted to see the slickness slide off of him like silk, leaving him naked for her.

"I'm the oldest and my mom and dad are like these goofy kids, so I haven't had much experience with that," he said.

Barbie moved closer to him. She could feel their heartbeats and breaths accelerating together, like one person, even though they weren't even touching. "Maybe you should get some," she said.

"Only if it's mutual," Todd said, reaching out to grasp her wrist.

It wasn't that Griffin was in love with Todd. Not exactly. Todd was obviously beautiful and appealed to men and women, gay and straight, with his silky jet black eyes and hair, high-carved cheekbones—which could not be disguised even by a stubbly growth of hair—and panther lope. Todd was rich and successful and talented—some people said "genius"—and he was generous with all of it, almost as if he were afraid if he didn't share everything he had, it would all be taken away, Griffin thought. But maybe Griffin was being too cynical, he told himself. Todd had a good heart, that was another thing about him. That was why he was such an appealing actor—you could feel his humanity even in the most mean-spirited roles. He made you understand and accept your darkness and then get beyond it.

But Griffin hadn't gotten beyond the dark feelings he had for Todd. Not love feelings, he told himself again. He just had a crush like everyone did, even the packs of straight guys that went to see Todd's movies and left imitating his walk or the way he held his cigarette.

He was Griffin's friend. His best friend. And his roommate. And now he was downstairs making out with one of the prettiest girls Griffin had ever seen. So it figures I feel freaked out, he thought.

He reached under the covers and touched his groin. Maybe if he came he wouldn't need to cry.

But sex, especially sex like this alone and hot more from shame than desire, wasn't going to do anything except make his sheets wet and his wrists ache. Besides, there was no one to think about. He never thought of Todd that way. It was more just the idea of Todd.

Griffin gave up and rolled over on his side. Suddenly he felt something bite his thigh. Fucking mosquitoes! But it wasn't the time of year.

Then Griffin Tyler heard the strangest thing he had ever heard in all his strange years.

"Hey, watch it!"

It was just a voice, but the highest, most

metallic little buzz of a voice, and weirdest of all, it was coming from under his blanket.

He threw the blanket aside and saw something nestling against his boxer shorts.

"What the fuck?"

"You could kill someone that way," Mab said, irate, as if he had intruded on her private boudoir. Which, actually, if you think about it, he had.

He hadn't thought he was that high. "Shit, Todd, what did you put in that pot, man?"

"I am not a hallucination, if that's what you're implying," Mab huffed.

"Yeah, right."

She grimaced at him, but her face was so small that he couldn't see the narrowing of her citrus-green eyes or the twist of her mouth. The only thing that gave away how pissed she was, was the tone of her voice.

"Yes. Correct."

"Well then, what are you?" he asked, figuring whatever he said would probably piss her off even more.

Actually, a question like this would usually have brought out the loathing in Mab, but this was, after all, the boy whose thigh she had been snuggling with and fanging for the last few moments, and she didn't choose her partners casually.

"None of the names you'd know are appropriate," she said (quite generously and graciously, she thought; he is a biscuit).

"Help me out a little here."

Mab sighed. The names made her queasy. But she'd do it for him. A girl had to be a little self-sacrificing when it came to the bedroom; it paid off in the long run. "Fairy. Brownie. Pixie. Pisky. (Ack! who thought of that.) Sprite. Nymph. (Nympho is more appropriate, quite honestly.) Will-o'-the-wisp. I find them all rather offensive."

Griffin knew the offensive aspect of labels. He didn't want to hurt her feelings, even if she were a hallucination. (Of course she was!) But she was so delicate—he could almost see right through her to the night sky in the window. And it was important to know. Strange things did exist.

"Well, if you're a real . . . whatever you are—prove it."

"All right. How about a little trip?" Mab asked.

"I thought that's what I was having."

"Not that kind."

Mab flew over to the window and looked down at the city shining below as if it were wet. Model-thin palm trees and ornate castle-type buildings, vintage cars with names like JACKAL and VERUCA, kids with flowery hair and large shoes eating spinach pies or reading at an outdoor café.

"This view sure beats the Valley," she murmured. Griffin came up behind her. Her wings were quivering with the lights and vibrations of the city. He wondered how they would feel brushing against his face. He tried to remember what the sensation had been like before he swatted his thigh. It didn't register as a mosquito bite anymore, but as something much more glamorous and exquisitely painful.

Mab glanced back at him. He blinked and rubbed his eyes.

"Come on!" she cried, pulling off the eucalyptus leaf bustier Barbie had made for her and whisking into the mock-orange-blossom and smog-scented night air.

Griffin hoisted himself up onto the sill and crawled out onto the ledge. He stood shakily, looking down below him. He'd imagined himself doing this a lot of times but it felt different now. His heart wasn't beating fast; he felt very calm, not even dizzy or anything.

"What the fuck," he said. "You only live once." Then he added, "I hope."

He hadn't thought Mab could hear, but there she was, flitting giddily around his hair, thinking how biscuitlike he was and how she would have given him his own pair of wings if she knew where to find them big enough. He'd look fabulous in them, and she couldn't say that about anyone she'd ever met. It bothered her, though, this thing about only wanting to live once. A boy like him should be ecstatic. So lovely and most certainly beloved, and out on a rather stinky but quite romantic night with a girl like herself.

"Very funny," she said. "We've got to do some work on that negative attitude of yours."

As Griffin teetered on the ledge like a novice tightrope walker, Mab, rather frantically—the serious nature of the situation had suddenly struck her—wove a starry web of light in the shape of a hammock. Griffin spread out his arms like a rock god in an MTV video and flung himself.

෴

In Todd's house Barbie and Todd were flying horizontally in front of the fireplace, their mouths tearing carnivorously, practically cannibalistically, at each other even though one of them was a vegan and the other had given up red meat.

Barbie paused, finally and pulled away, thinking she might have to wear very dark lipstick the next day to hide the bruises.

"I get scared sometimes," she said.

Todd's voice was tender, dry, so different from the kisses, although they were tender, too, even in their ferocity. "Just tell me," he whispered.

Mab and Griffin, supported by her web of light, flew through the dark sky. His laughter was as silvered and buoyant as her web.

"Just don't try this at home, kids," Mab said.

Todd, slowly, gently, took off Barbie's shirt, running his fingers over her body as if he had never seen a girl naked before.

"Is this okay?" he asked.

She nodded, too out of breath to speak.

When she tried to take off his T-shirt he moved her hands away.

Griffin chased Mab in hoop-de-hoops and loop-de-loops. He took off his shirt and watched it fall as the cool air caressed his body.

Todd and Barbie rolled over and over each other on the floor like children on a grassy hill in summer, not afraid of where they would land.

Mab, her wings beating furiously, hovered above Griffin as he closed his eyes and dove through the clouds.

And so these sets of lovers (because for Mab and Griffin this was lovemaking, too) flickered, melding and merging, one into the other, bodies entwined wings that burn in the night and will soon cool to mirror dawn.

In the morning Todd and Barbie were asleep by the fireplace.

In the room upstairs, Griffin and Mab lay sleeping, too. She was curled up by his neck. His breath was making her wings wave back and forth like petals in a breeze. They were both smiling beatifically. Except for his boxer shorts printed with Goofy, he looked like an androgynous young angel in an old Italian painting.

Suddenly, the doorbell chimed, echoing through the house, and disturbing the peace that had settled over everything within it like the loose glitter from Mab's wings. Griffin and Mab woke right away. With uncharacteristic shyness she realized she was half naked and disappeared behind a potted African violet that Todd had received from a lovestruck fan and forgotten about, and that Griffin was nursing back to health.

Griffin got out of bed, rubbing his eyes, trying to remember the strange and fantastical dream that he'd had. He stumbled downstairs past Barbie and Todd asleep on the floor. The feelings from the night before came back. If only he could remember that dream better, he thought. All that was left was a sort of tingling sensation along his naked spine and the phantom scent of honeysuckle—or something—on his fingers.

The doorbell clanged again.

"Just a minute!" Griffin called, his bare toes curling up with cold on the parquet floor of the entry hall as he went to answer.

He opened the door for a silicone-enhanced young girl who would have been beautiful if not for the look of fury and disgust contorting her face.

"Hi, Ashley," Griffin said.

Sometimes he wondered if she even remembered his name.

"Where's Todd?" She pushed past him into the house. He could almost feel a chill in the air where she'd been.

"You slut! You've always taken what belongs to me!"

Griffin came in to see Ashley standing over Todd and Barbie.

"Ashley, calm down," Todd said, sheltering Barbie with his back and putting his hands up to his chest. He was still wearing his T-shirt.

"Fuck you! Did you get her name tattooed on your chest yet?"

"Listen, calm down and then we'll talk."

"I don't have anything to say to you. I just wanted to come and see for myself what *hos* you both are."

Ashley turned and marched out. Her platforms echoed through the house like horse's hooves. Barbie wrapped herself in a blanket and stood up. She was noticing how Todd's hands were still on his chest.

"I can't believe I stayed with you," she said, as angry at herself as at him. After all, she'd known about Ashley. But Todd could make you forget a lot of things with his eyes and his hands and his voice and his house full of angels and gargoyles.

"She's not my girlfriend," he said. He knew he was digging it deeper now but he had to say something. "She just kind of attached herself to me."

Like everyone you meet and look at with those gluey eyes, Barbie thought. "I wonder why!" she said.

"What does that mean?"

"It seems like you encourage a lot of people to get attached." She looked over at Griffin standing by the door. Sad-eyed. She couldn't believe she was here like this in front of him. How many girls came in and out of Todd's hotel every week? "And what's this about tattoos?"

She pulled Todd's T-shirt up before he could stop her. Even the gleaming brown perfection of his chest could not distract her from the elaborate letters scrawled across it.

The letters read: SARAH FOREVER.

And the letters read: LISA FOREVER.

And the letters said: NINA FOREVER.

THIS GIRL, NEVER, Barbie thought. She grabbed her things and left the room. If she had been wearing her shoes she would have stomped as hard and loud as Ashley, clomping out.

Todd looked at Griffin. "Fuck! What did I do?" he said with the bewilderment that always overtook him in these situations. He really couldn't understand how his genuine appreciation of ladies could cause so much trouble. As far as he saw it, they all should be worshiped and have their names permanently branded on flesh; it was just that he couldn't accommodate each one the way she deserved. And then he would meet another. . . .

And now he had met Barbie onto whose slim body he would have liked to tattoo himself.

But Griffin, who understood each girl better than the last, only shook his head and walked out, too.

Todd collapsed on the couch and raked his fingernails over his chest.

Later, he and Griffin were eating their organic oat flakes and chocolate rice milk out of soup tureens that were as inappropriately large for cereal as the hotel kitchen was for the two young men who shared it.

"I really fucked up," Todd said, referring, of course, not to the size of his kitchen or cereal bowl, but to Barbie, whose face he was afraid he'd see, magically painted there under the flakes and milk.

Griffin, who had a better chance of seeing Mab in his cereal bowl because of her size, said, "You just don't think about what you're doing, Todd."

"I don't want to hurt anyone." Todd put down his bowl before the bottom was uncovered.

Griffin shrugged his bare light shoulders heavily. It seemed simple to him. "Well then, don't."

"You can't help it if someone goes for you," Todd said. He knew this was a weak response, but he felt like he had to say something to defend himself. Even if Barbie's accusing eyes weren't in his cereal tureen, Griffin's were staring at him hard across the table.

"Were you born with that ego or did it just develop over time?"

Todd jumped up. He wanted to smash his tureen like a scene in a movie but decided he'd broken too many plates lately. "What's up with you, man?" he said. "I think you need to get laid or something."

As soon as he'd said it, Todd felt like he'd broken something inside of Griffin who stood up and dumped the rest of his cereal into the sink.

"Fuck you."

"Griff," Todd said, "just chill, man."

Griffin went to the swinging door and stopped, looked back at Todd. Suddenly, the dream he'd had—or whatever it was—had come back to him. He felt the cool shiver of Mab's web caressing his body as he floated through space, turning like a baby in the womb. He stared into Todd's eyes that seemed so much less dark, strange, and inviting than the sky Mab had showed him.

"What happened to me last night so beats getting laid. . . ."

"I'd like to try that," Todd said gently.

Griffin shrugged again and pushed through

the doors that swung behind him like large wooden wings.

Barbie knew she should get a cab but she didn't have the energy to stop and call one so she just kept walking. Not even realizing she was doing it, she dragged her knuckles against a brick wall until they were flecked with blood. Ever since she was eleven she would surprise herself with bleeding—nicks on her fingers, bitten tongue. Mab would waken her, as if from a trance and she would see what she had done.

"You're destroying your hands," Mab said.

Barbie looked down calmly at her tattered knuckles. "I thought you didn't care what I did," she said, too tired to even wonder at Mab's sudden appearance.

"Well, you are kind of an imbecile. Why did you leave him like that? I wanted to stay for breakfast." She paused as if she were sniffing something delectable and buttery and sweet on the air. "Biscuits and jam. Croissants. Eclairs."

"Since when do you have such a big appetite?" Barbie asked.

Mab shrugged her fragile, winged shoulders, stretched her arms above her head and grinned demonically so that her vampiric incisors showed. Barbie shook her head with disapproval.

"What did you do, Mab? You are so bad."

"I know how to enjoy myself," Mab said. "Unlike you." She had slipped downstairs after Griffin and witnessed the drama from inside a dusty arrangement of fake roses that was still making her nose tickle. "Why'd you give him such a hard time? You knew he and Ashley had a thing going."

"I wasn't sure if they still did," said Barbie. "And anyway, he didn't handle it well. He's some kind of control freak."

"Who bit *your* butt? Or should I say, didn't he bite your butt the way you like?"

"You're just so funny," Barbie said, lighting a cigarette.

Mab coughed. That was all she needed after the dust blossoms. And besides, this masochistic trip was getting carried a little too far. "You really shouldn't smoke so much, you know," she said.

"Since when did you care? You're starting to sound like the crocodile. Very concerned about cigarette smoke. But leave your eleven-year-old with a child molester? Now that's cool."

Barbie stopped walking and put her bleeding knuckles in her mouth. Then she sat down on the sidewalk, dropped her head, closed her eyes, bit her lip, and pressed her palms against her ears as if she could make the memories go away like the monkeys who refused to acknowledge evil.

It didn't work. She saw the three monkeys. They all had Hamilton Waverly's face.

"What brought this up again?" Mab asked. Her voice was less shrill now, whispering into Barbie's ear as she tickled Barbie's neck with her wings.

"I saw him."

Using all her strength, Mab wrestled the cigarette out of Barbie's hand and let it fall into the gutter where it sputtered embers and then ash. Barbie glared at her and almost reached for it, threw up her hands, stood, and started walking. Mab flew into her purse and held on to the rim, staring up and not even saying a word of protest as Barbie lit another cigarette.

Barbie tried to sneak into the house

through the back, figuring her mother would still be asleep, but Mrs. Marks had decided to start soaking up rays early. She was lying on her stomach by the pool like some kind of beached sea mammal. She sat up when she saw Barbie, holding her bathing-suit top up over her greased breasts.

"And where have you been all night?"

Barbie just hopped up the Astroturf steps into the house. Mrs. Marks struggled to fasten her bathing-suit top, remembering vaguely how much easier life was when there was a man around to do things like that.

She went inside and pounded on her daughter's door with her fist.

"Let me in," she shouted.

"I told you, my career is over," Barbie shouted back through the door. "So I don't think we have anything left to say to each other."

"You cannot stay here if you're going to behave like this."

Barbie, who was crouched on her bed holding up the book of the two girl photographers and their Mabs like a shield, said, "Fine."

"I don't see how you plan on leaving."

"I've made enough money in the last five

years to buy my own house. And this one too, probably."

"Not without my permission."

Barbie threw down the book and lunged at the door. She almost fell into her mother's coconut-greased arms as it opened. "It's my money!" she screamed.

"I'm not going to speak to you if that's going to be your attitude."

"Don't, then." Barbie clenched her fists so that her fingernails dug tiny half moons into her palms.

Her mother seemed suddenly calm, like a fat cat who had swallowed a parakeet. "I was going to tell you about New York," she said sweetly. Barbie could almost hear Emily parakeet's mangled feathers in her throat.

"What. About. New. York."

"We've been offered a show there."

"You've never let me go before," Barbie said.

Mrs. Marks nodded and swallowed. Barbie couldn't help imagining Emily sliding down her mother's gullet. "Well I'm just going to have to get over my fear of flying for this. It's an important opportunity. And you deserve it."

"I'm not going anywhere with you."

But Mrs. Marks acted as if she hadn't heard her. "And I thought we'd let you keep the money from this one. In your own account. Think about it."

She walked away. Barbie could almost see a fat furry tail swinging savagely from her bathing-suit butt and a trail of feathers left behind. She went back into her room and shut the door. Mab was doing acrobatics on the rung in the bird cage.

"'And I thought we'd let you *keep* the money from this one. In your own *account!* *Think* about it!' You've outviled yourself, Crocodile."

"I'm not going."

Mab stopped swinging and glared at her. "Of course you are. You've always wanted to go to New York."

"Not with her."

"We'll ditch her."

"You mean you'd go?"

"Of course. I'm sick of the Valley. I need some culture. And so do you."

To emphasize the point she did a perfect flip over the bird-cage rung. She, for one, wouldn't have any problem with flying, Barbie thought.

But Mrs. Marks did. She was gulping down a martini and the color had drained from her face—you could tell even with her tan and thick makeup. At the slightest turbulence she would hit her call button repeatedly.

"What's that? Stewardess, what was that?"

"Can I help you, ma'am?" The flight attendant's smile looked painted on. Barbie wondered if she were going to slap her mother.

"What was that?" Mrs. Marks said.

"Just some slight turbulence, maam. Can I get you anything?"

"Another pillow. If you can call it that." She dug her fingernails into the tiny thing. "It looks like a Maxi pad."

Barbie couldn't help smiling. It almost sounded like something Mab would say. In fact, she could feel the tiniest vibration of laughter in her purse, like a beeper going off, where Mab was hiding.

The flight attendant tucked another Maxi pad behind Mrs. Marks's head, smiled, waited. There wasn't going to be a thank-you. She pivoted on her pumps and walked away.

"They all wish they were models but they weren't pretty enough so they have to take this God-awful job."

Barbie rolled her eyes. She looked into her purse. Mab rolled her eyes too.

Later, when Mrs. Marks had passed out over her last martini, Barbie sat staring out the tiny plane window into the darkness. She heard something stirring in her purse.

"Give me a sip of that," Mab said.

Barbie held her ginger ale over her bag and started to pour a drop down to Mab whose wings, in the reading light, looked as phosphorescent as the soda.

"Not that! The martini!"

"Since when do you drink?"

"Since I started flying."

"You're always flying."

"Yes, in the natural way. This is hideous."

"You sound like the crocodile."

The flight attendant walked by, heard Barbie talking to her purse, and gave her a forced oh-great-trapped-with-another-looney smile. Barbie smiled back at her and picked up a book.

"Well, you *look* like her!" Mab shouted up from the bottom of the purse. Before Barbie could protest she said, "Oh, I think I'm going to . . ."

There was the sound of a tiny retch.

"Mab?"

She flew out of the purse, wiping her mouth daintily with the back of her hand, and into Barbie's carry-on bag. Barbie grimaced into her purse. She took the airsick bag out of the seat pocket in front of her.

"Have you ever heard of a barf bag?" she said, holding it so Mab could see.

"Yes, Pigeon. And now you have your very own personal genuine vinyl one."

Meanwhile, Todd was sitting on his wrought-iron balcony, smoking a cigarette, squinting through his sunglasses into the palm-tree haze and thinking about Barbie. She was all he thought about. Todd couldn't help writing the names of the girls he'd loved on his body. It was almost as if they wrote themselves there when he made love with them. Well, that was one way to explain it, anyway. But he did become infatuated so easily. And it wasn't just physical beauty. Although he was a master connoisseur of that—the colt legs, the way the muscles tensed along the inner thigh (Nina); the lips, the way they swelled a little, the long ballerina neck (Sarah); the plush breasts pushing against the lace of a bra (Lisa). But when those things were combined with sweetness (Nina took in kittens with leukemia); or sadness (Sarah had to wear a back brace in junior high for scoliosis and the boys made fun of her so she was still shy around them); or some funny talent like polishing her toenails with the brush in her teeth (Lisa); he became deeply smitten.

Todd had grown up in Northern California in a big ranch house called Love Farm, with five brothers and sisters. His parents had an antiquarian book shop called The Book of Love and grew all their own organic vegetables. They encouraged their children to put on plays for them after dinner—TV did not exist at Love Farm. Todd was the oldest, and everyone knew he would become a big star, possibly on the TV none of them watched, although his parents often cautioned him about the dangers of Hollywood; they had met there on a chewing-gum commercial, fallen instantly in love over a single piece of gum (shared), and decided to get out while they were still relatively unscarred by the business.

Todd's expansive, loving, freewheeling nature was encouraged. He smoked pot and discussed the Beat poets with his parents; he ran through the woods with his brothers and sisters, leading them at games of Indians and Indians (no one would be the Cowboys); he wrote the plays they performed at night, soliciting the services of the girls in the neighborhood to inhabit the role of leading lady. The plays were always romantic and ended with a passionate kiss, much to the dismay of Todd's younger siblings, who found it all particularly stomach-turning. But Todd's audience and his co-stars enjoyed the romance. And of course, so did Todd, who felt privately that his calling in life was to kiss as many girls as possible and let even more watch him doing it so they could live vicariously through the ones on screen.

It wasn't that he had such a huge ego. He really did feel that he had a certain healing effect, and this was, in fact, somewhat true. But until he'd met Barbie he hadn't realized how his actions could become so hurtful as to cancel out any healing. He knew that it wasn't worth anything if it caused her to leave him like that. She had the sweetness and sadness and quirky talent of all his ex-loves combined.

Todd decided, in that way he had—so self-assured, although a pissed-off ex might have said cocky—that he would find Barbie. After a long search employing the Net and various people who worked for him, he was able to ascertain that she was in New York City at a certain very elegant hotel and that she would be checking in on a Thursday evening at around 8:00 P.M.

If Los Angeles is a woman reclining billboard model and the San Fernando Valley is her teenybopper sister, then New York is their cousin. Her hair is dyed autumn red or aubergine or Egyptian henna, depending on her mood. Her skin is pale as frost and she wears beautiful Jil Sander suits and Prada pumps on which she walks faster than a speeding taxi (when it is caught in rush hour, that is). Her lips are some unlikely shade of copper or violet, courtesy of her local MAC drag queen makeup consultant.

She is always carrying bags of clothes, bouquets of roses, take-out Chinese containers, or bagels. Museum tags fill her pockets and purses, along with perfume samples and invitations to art gallery openings. When she is walking to work, to ward off bums or psychos, her face resembles the Statue of Liberty, but at home in her candlelit, dove-colored apartment, the stony look fades away and she smiles like the sterling roses she has bought for herself to make up for the fact that she is single and her feet are sore.

This was what Barbie was thinking as she, her mother and Mab—carefully hidden away, of course—drove in a taxi through the streets of Manhattan on the way to their hotel. The speed, color, noise, glitter (shop windows, bar signs) and burning smells (hot dogs, engines) were all almost too much. The only way she could think about it, take it in, was to make New York a woman, one she wished she could photograph. She reached into her bag, carefully avoiding the sleeping Mab, and fondled the camera Todd Range had given to her from the Adam and Eve cabinet.

The hotel had a huge lobby with an inlaid marble floor, starry lamps, and an arrangement of flowers twice as big as Barbie. She wondered if any Mabs lived there. They would have been quite the sophisticated Mabs, dressed in the slightly metallic pollen of exotic star-gazer lilies, supping on the champagne of lily nectars and admiring the Armani-clad rears of international biscuit businessmen, as Mab was doing from inside Barbie's bag.

Their room was decorated in rose and gold with flocked *fleur-de-lis* wallpaper. The toilet paper was wrapped up like expensive gifts and the towels smelled liked warm baked cakes. Mrs. Marks bathed and then lay on the bed with a towel turban and a green facial mask, eating a four-course room service dinner with a heavy silver fork and watching the shopping channel on the vast TV. Barbie sat at the window, staring out into the city. She couldn't believe she was stuck inside with it just waiting out there like a courtesan reclining for her prince. Well, maybe that wasn't quite the right image. A crazy man was howling like a wolf at the moon. There were sirens.

The courtesan was more like a harem of slightly deranged, though vibrant, prostitutes of every imaginable ethnicity, dressed in designer rags from garbage bins.

Barbie and Mab didn't speak, of course, because of their roommate, but if they had they would have discovered that they were sharing the same secret fantasy in which disgruntled model and her feisty winged companion meet dark-eyed gen-X matinée idol and androgynous boy beauty and frolic through the streets of a toxic and intoxicating city.

In the morning, the fantasy began to come true.

Barbie and her mother were leaving their keys with the desk attendant in the lobby when Barbie noticed two young men in sunglasses checking in to a room. Her heart slammed.

It was Todd and Griffin.

Todd turned and winked at her over the top of his sunglasses.

"Come on, Barbie," her mother said.

Todd grinned like he was auditioning to play a suave and debonair young devil. He pointed to the ground and then raised ten fingers. She turned her back on him, but when she felt him slip a piece of paper into her hand, she took it, and followed her mother out through the revolving glass doors into the spinning light.

In the cab she read the note:

I'M SO SORRY I HURT YOU.

Presumptuous egotist, she thought.

I GOT THOSE DONE WHEN I WAS YOUNG . . .

"Those," meaning the tattoos. As if he thought she'd know right away what he was talking about. As if she'd been thinking about it this whole time. Well, she did know, but . . .

. . . AND EVEN STUPIDER.

That was true.

PLEASE FORGIVE ME. YOU'RE ALL I THINK ABOUT. —TODD

Okay, charming. And he had come all this way. To see her, supposedly. Quite the operator. But she was smiling anyway; she couldn't help it.

And in spite of the bumpy cab ride, the stuffy purse, and the close proximity of Crocodile, so was Mab.

At René Rothberg's studio Barbie tried to keep still while the young assistant pinned the pale-yellow charmeuse satin gown to fit her. It was difficult because of Mab who was wriggling around under the drape of the cowl neckline.

"You better be nice to him!" a voice said.

Barbie had to resist swatting her neck.

"What was that?" asked the assistant, pins sticking out of her mouth like surreal and dangerous tiny silver fangs.

"Nothing. Um. You're so nice and trim." It really wasn't the best choice of a cover-up line. The assistant frowned at Barbie's jutting hipbones.

"Sure. Thanks. So are you."

Barbie adjusted her cowl.

"Could you please keep still?" the assistant said, as sharp as the pins in her mouth.

"Sorry," said Barbie.

"You know I hate that," said Mab, who had never gotten over her disgust with apologies—especially the unwarranted ones that Barbie was still prone to after years of useless correcting.

"Shhh!" Barbie said.

"What?" said the assistant, *who must think I'm some kind of junkie freak by now,* Barbie thought.

"Nothing," she said. And then, in spite of the twitching inside of her dress, added, "Sorry."

The rest of the day was a silky whirlwind punctured with the threat of pins. It was blinding lights, sweat, breasts, glossy thighs, pinching fingers as René Rothberg fussed with his creations. It was too much for Mab, who took shelter somewhere in a bouquet of roses to watch the naked models and critique their bodies to herself. (She felt her proportions were much better, as well as the shade and texture of her skin.) Barbie managed to get through it by trancing out on the lovely colors of the dresses that reminded her of some cosmic breeds of flowers, and to count down the hours until she would see Todd.

When she stepped out of the elevator at 10:10—she had forced herself to be a little late—he wasn't there. Shit, she thought, I should have had another cigarette. Waiting would only make her seem more vulnerable.

But then she felt hot forearms circling her waist. He had stepped out from behind a potted plant, with Griffin behind him.

"What are you guys doing in New York?" she said. She had practiced this line a few times, trying to sound annoyed, but it came out more like a little girl at a surprise party.

"I have my ways of getting information," said Todd from behind the upturned collar of his coat, every bit the sleuthster.

"It's a *celebrity* thing." Griffin rolled his eyes at the secret-agent act.

"I'm so glad you're here!" Barbie, realizing how she sounded, took out her cigarettes. "You know. It's boring with just my mom to hang with."

Someone from inside Barbie's beaded bag made an "A-hem!" noise. Barbie gave the shimmering glass flowers a dirty look.

"How'd you ditch her?" Todd asked.

"She's out."

"You mean, like out on the town?"

"No. Like passed out."

Todd grinned, then straightened his collar and gloves. Now he was the gentleman escort, the perfect date who, when he held your hand, could show you Ozzes, Wonderlands, and Magic Planets. "Cool. So what do you want to do?"

They practically skipped down the streets. Barbie felt as if she might take off into the air on invisible Mabish wings. The night was a rush of steaming pasta, wet irises, Italian leathers, swaddled beggars, skulking boys, sulking girls, garbage piles, pretzel vendors.

Todd leapt out into the traffic and hailed a cab, into which they piled, on top of each other, like circus clowns. Barbie leaned out the window, trying to sense the stories in the air as they sped uptown. She wished she had her camera. The pictures she would take would be streaked with melting rainbows and spangled with sequin lights.

The Metropolitan Museum was a palace. Barbie thought about the museum in Los Angeles, uneven and rambling and built on pits of tar where a stone baby mastodon stood on the bank watching his mother drown. The two buildings like the two cities. She followed Todd and Griffin out of the cab and up the steep gray stone steps.

Inside, Barbie felt like Alice, shrinking before the enormous stone Buddha (if the Giants were like him—so beatific and tender—she would never have minded being one) and growing before the tiny earringed cats that the Egyptians put in their tombs. She, Todd and Griffin (not to mention a certain small and hidden fourth party) bowed to Buddhas and walked in profile, Egyptian-style, past friezes of flat-footed beauties in elaborate headdresses and sheer skimpy skirts. In the Greek and Roman rooms of pale marbles, Barbie was paying homage to a statue of Aphrodite decked with doves while Griffin, from the corner of his eye, took in the form of a young nude Adonis. Todd came up behind Barbie and clutched her waist so that she jumped.

"What are you dreaming about?" he asked.

"I wonder if she liked having her portrait done," Barbie said, nodding to Aphrodite and thinking of a certain giant bird cage from a long time ago, "or if she wanted to be a sculptor herself."

Todd kissed her cheek and she felt the comforting scratch of his stubble. "There's a photo exhibit I want you to see."

It was Diane Arbus, in the downstairs gallery—a row of haunted black and white faces staring out at them—slack-jawed, saint-eyed.

"Aren't they amazing?" Todd said.

Barbie wondered if Todd were thinking about the camera he had given her, trying to inspire her. And was that for her, or something to do with this thing he had about being a patron of the arts?

But Griffin wasn't thinking about his ego at all, she could tell by the way he stood so close to the pictures, his face, under the thick black-framed glasses he'd put on, unconsciously mirroring the strange sad expressions.

"I don't want this to sound wrong, but they're not quite human-looking you know? I mean that as a good thing. They're like . . ." he hesitated, trying to remember the funny word he didn't think he'd known before—"piskies or something."

"Piskies?" Todd said, using the tone he often took for Griffin—affectionate but a tiny bit condescending.

"You know. Fairies or whatever."

Todd shrugged. "Oh. Yeah."

Barbie had been cringing since Griffin had used the "p" word, so she wasn't even surprised when she heard the tiny voice coming out of her bag. "I am *much* more beautiful than that!"

Todd glanced around. "What?"

Barbie cleared her throat. "What?"

"What did you just . . ."

"I didn't say anything."

Todd cocked his head like a dog and rubbed his ear. "I've got to stop listening to music so loud."

Griffin only frowned, wondering if you could have dream flashbacks that were this real.

To ground themselves they decided they should get something to eat. In Manhattan, Todd told Barbie, you could have any cuisine you could imagine, from Native American buffalo to sticky macrobiotic mochi rice-flour waffles. She asked for vegan so they headed downtown again, to a restaurant decorated like an enchanted forest with cascades of vines hanging from the ceiling and real birds perched on branches. Their table was a tree stump on which the waiter, clad in a sheer green voile shirt and green satin bellbottoms, placed exotic alcohol-free herbal fruit drinks decorated with paper parasols. Barbie snatched her parasol and dropped it discreetly into the beaded purse, where Mab caught it, pushed it open and twirled it delicately above her head.

When Barbie saw Griffin staring at the top of her bag and then rubbing his eyes, she quickly pointed to the rainbow colors twinkling through the network of branches. "Trippy lights. They could make you hallucinate."

Todd sipped his drink. "I feel like I'm hallucinating this whole night."

"Maybe it's the flower essences you're drinking."

"I mean that I'm seeing you again." His eyes caught her, so that it was hard for her to breathe. "I was afraid I wouldn't after the other night."

Barbie tried to look away. "You almost didn't."

"What made you change your mind?"

"I didn't have a choice. You kind of just appeared."

"I had to see you."

It amazed her how he could talk like this

with others around. Well, with *Griffin* around—he didn't know about Mab, and the rest of the people in the restaurant were absorbed with their mung bean casseroles or the waterfall that was flicking drops onto their faces as they ate. But Griffin was looking away now, as if he hadn't heard Todd. Or as if he's heard this a million times before, Barbie thought.

The waiter brought the first course—huge platters of exotic root vegetables—lotus root, burdock, taro, ginger cooked in a sesame sauce.

"There aren't any good places like this in L.A.," said Barbie.

"How long have you not eaten meat?" Todd was trying to wrestle the unwieldy wheel of lotus up to his mouth with his chopsticks.

"Five years. When I was little I would never eat baby animals and then I just stopped eating any. One day I just couldn't anymore." She stopped, feeling suddenly queasy, and was thankful no one was having hot dogs anywhere in the near vicinity. "My mom had a cow. No pun intended." Thinking of her mother, she checked her watch under which her pulse had started to accelerate. "God. I better get back."

"Not yet," Todd said. "There's somewhere else I want to take you."

A life-size Barbie and Ken in wedding clothes stood on top of an enormous wedding cake in the middle of the night club dance floor. As the trip-hop music beat the dancers into a frenzy, Barbie and Ken turned to each other and kissed, then began to rip off each other's clothes like two dolls that had spent about forty years waiting to do more than smile placidly at each other and were suddenly not only mobile, but bestowed with the proper equipment to consummate their relationship.

All around the club were more tableaux featuring the famous pair and their friends. Barbie and Todd grooved under a toy dream house like the one Mab used as her spa. Mab, fascinated that anyone would want to fetish-ize the plastic objects that were always trying to outdo her or get in her way, had boldly ventured out of her companion's purse and, disguised as one of the disco lights, was hover-ing near Griffin. She was close enough to smell the cigarette smoke and vanilla shampoo of his hair and see the beads of perspiration on his temples. They made her think sentimentally of dewdrops, which she had never cared that much for, but which now, in this terribly urban environment, had a special appeal.

A tall, handsome man dressed as a Magic-Earring Ken approached Griffin. Mab shuddered to herself. The man had on orange-ish makeup that made him look just like the doll.

"Haven't I seen you in that jeans ad?" he asked.

Griffin shrugged. "I guess."

"Want to dance?"

"No!" Mab almost shouted, disgusted. She wanted to bite Ken's perfectly straight orange nose. She would have, too, if Griffin hadn't said, "No thanks, man."

"Come on. All you have to do is stand there and shuffle your feet."

Griffin hesitated. He reminded Barbie of the deer she had seen in *National Geographic*—like he would bolt away at any moment, but with something still trusting in his eyes. Ken took his hand and pulled him onto the dance floor.

It was too much for Mab, who started to target Ken, but then decided she might take a sweeter revenge for herself and buzzed at Griffin, landing on his bare wrist and sinking her fangs into the thin skin there.

"Ow! Fuck!" he shouted, swatting at the place where Mab had been (she was now watching from behind his ear).

"What's wrong?" Ken asked.

"Something bit me."

Ken grinned and licked his lips. "Sounds exciting."

Griffin stopped dancing and walked away. Ken followed him. He held up the plastic necklace he was wearing. It was a round ring on a cord.

"Can you believe they actually got away with making a kid's doll like this?"

Griffin tried to ignore him but he kept following.

"They thought it was a new-wave necklace!"

"Yeah," Griffin said. Mab felt bad that she'd bitten him. She wished she'd gotten Ken instead, even if she'd have to spit him out rather than enjoy the delectable taste of her favorite biscuit.

"You know what it really is, don't you?" Ken smirked, and Mab, who'd once made Barbie buy her some porno magazines—purely for research purposes—suddenly recognized the ring and realized what Ken wanted to put in it. Griffin didn't seem to, but he was out of there anyway.

"Okay. Yeah. I gotta go. See ya," he said.

He went over to Todd and Barbie who were dancing close together under the dream house, sweat sliding over their bodies in a delicate disco-lit sheen.

"Todd," said Griffin.

There was no response. Mab wondered if she'd have to bite Todd now. She couldn't stand to see Griffin stressed out. Maybe she could whisk him away from there in her silvery, glistering web.

"Todd!"

Todd stopped dancing.

"It's 3:30." Mab's biscuit pressed a thumb against his throbbing temple.

Barbie woke from the Todd-trance she had fallen into. "The crocodile will strangle me," she said.

᮫

Mab was floating on a bar of soap as if it were a raft, in the slightly murky swimming pool that was Barbie's bath.

"She is such a croc," Barbie said.

Mrs. Marks had not caught her coming home from her first excursion, but the night after the fashion show, when Barbie had slipped out to be with Todd, her mother had found out and changed the plane tickets so they would be leaving early.

"I'm going to take you home where I can keep an eye on you," she had said.

"Yeah. A croc of shit!" said Mab now. "So what? Let her go back to the Valley. We can stay here."

Barbie rubbed the pumice stone over a callus on her heel. "I can't, Mab."

Mab frowned. "Why not?" She didn't need this show of cowardice. Plus she had the headache from hell from drinking champagne in Todd and Griffin's suite the night before while Todd and Barbie made out. Griffin had never even come home.

"Where would I stay?" said Barbie. "I don't have any money."

Mab touched her own toes, which were, she was proud to say, callus-free. Wings really helped in that way. "It's time for you to grow up," she said. "You could change your name to something like . . ." she paused. "Selena. I think it means something to do with the moon. You could become a photographer and take pictures of me."

"I can't. All I know how to do is model."

Mab scowled at her. It seemed hopeless to try to reform the thought patterns that this stubborn creature insisted on clinging to. And after years of free therapy! It really was a shame. "Well, I'm staying."

"You can't stay here by yourself."

"Why not?" Mab scoffed. "This is a fabulous city."

"What about Mr. Biscuit?"

Mab was annoyed Barbie would bring up Griffin now. He was definitely her weak spot. But she couldn't let him keep her from getting on with her life. She had places to go, people to meet. It was clear to her now. She couldn't be selfish anymore. She had the gift of her presence to share with the world.

"He's a biscuit-lover, I told you," she said, trying to convince herself, just as much as Barbie, that she had to let him go. "Besides," she added, "I'm sick of watching you get all the attention. I'm destined for fame."

"If you come back I can learn to take your picture and make you famous."

But Mab couldn't believe that one anymore. "How long have you been promising me? You don't even know how to use a camera." She knew this was hurting but now, realizing that she and Barbie were really going to be apart, for the first time in so many years, she couldn't stop. Maybe this would somehow make the separation easier. "I think you're right, Pigeon. Maybe all you can do is mope around in front of the camera and complain about the crocodile."

Barbie swallowed soapy-tasting tears. "You are so mean, Mab."

"And you are such the bore."

Mab slipped off the bar of soap into the water, rinsed herself and then rose into the air, shaking and flinging droplets everywhere. She flew to the hotel window, where she paused, only briefly, before taking off into the vast, rumbling, stinking planet of a city that she hoped somehow to conquer.

While Barbie's plane flew through the smoggy skies of Los Angeles, what looked like an insect was flitting through the air of Manhattan, an insect camouflaged by its own brilliance and dazzle-beauty in a city where shop windows shone with diamonds and gauze, where confetti fell from open windows, where lovers in horse-drawn carriages tossed bouquets into the sky.

Barbie was moving plastic furniture around in the dollhouse. She found a book of matches. *Father: no attention,* someone had written, in letters so small they were almost indecipherable. Did I write that? she wondered. Am I losing my mind?

The insect, that was actually a girl, was writing her name, as big as she possibly could, on a phone booth, hoping that if people saw it often enough they would begin to discuss the phenomenon of the return of the queen. They would begin to search for her. At which time she would make herself available to them, and like some magic silver thread, she would transform the coarse, dull fabric of their lives.

Barbie was holding the matchbook, trying not to cry. The phone rang. Barbie answered, knowing it was not the long distance call she'd been hoping for. How could it be? Someone as small as her friend couldn't lift a receiver off its hook and would be too proud to ask anyone for help.

If the friend were there, the phone call would have made Barbie run to the bathroom to put on lipstick and perfume and whirl around asking the bitchy friend "How do I look?" knowing that the best response she could possibly get would be "Your head is too large," but this would not have bothered her because she was going to see Todd. It was Todd. But the friend was not there, the mean little snippity friend with the supernatural wings and the effervescent internal light by which you could read books in bed, when you were supposed to be asleep. So even Todd's call did not entice Barbie to get up.

"Hi, Todd," she said dully. "My mom made me go home early. . . . I just don't feel like going out right now. . . . Nothing. I'm just a little depressed. . . . No, it's okay. I'll call you some time. . . . Okay, 'bye."

It was all she could manage to say. How could she tell him what was really wrong? Telling him about what happened when she was little, about Mab—it was almost the same thing. They would have both frightened him. She hung up the phone and opened the book with the pictures of the two young photographers and their Mabs. A dried purple jacaranda flower fell out of it, like a discarded, shriveled bonnet. Barbie held it up to the light and saw the veins stand out against the fragile, papery petals.

Mab. Flying along a crowded street in the garment district of Manhattan. Trucks. Ramps. Racks of clothing rolling along at breakneck speed. Breakneck as in: could break the neck of someone who stands five feet five inches let alone pinkie-sized. Mab. Bedraggled and miserable. A homeless man in the gutter with his head in his hands and a sign that read HAVE AIDS PLEASE HELP propped up against his deteriorating shins. Mab targeted a wealthy-looking fat-cat business man and wrestled the wallet from his pocket with her thief's-dream fingers. She let it drop into the homeless man's lap. He didn't look up. As she was about to brush her wings like a kiss across his cheek, she was almost squashed by a skateboard from hell. She turned and gave it the finger as it roared off into the distance. But her finger was so small it wasn't a very effective gesture.

Now it was Teeny of the Valley who had lost her Mab, just like Sis before her. The Teenybopper has lost her bop—the bop in her walk, her pocket-bop. She no longer parks her VW in the liquor-store parking lot on hot nights to dance to the radio with her friends, loping around and swinging their arms like the punk-rock boys. She no longer passes joints back and forth out of her car window while speeding down the high-way, almost causing a collision with the truckful of pothead surfers. She no longer paints her fingernails with the toxic blue glitter and makes what she calls "mouth-condoms" out of her bubble gum, encasing her tongue in the thin plasticky sheath. She has given up dancing on the train tracks, breaking into used-car lots to see herself in that icy silver blue light, given up on stealing lipstick and eating hard candy Sweet Tarts for breakfast. Depressed, she stays in her room listening to the hot wind jostling the trees and skittering the garbage down the street. She has even stopped listening to her music. Most of her favorite singers have o.d.'d anyway. She stares up at the posters of the young, beautiful, and dead on her wall. Something is missing, but she already can't quite remember what it is.

What it is is a Mab. It seems as if without her the whole Valley will catch on fire or collapse into itself in an earthquake. The whole world is burning with hot winds and smog and exhaust. The flowers are all dying off except for the poison oleanders. The trees with the upside-down bell-shaped yellow flowers that once reminded Teeny of Mab's closet full of prom dresses have all shed the blossom gowns. The mini-malls are staggering across the land like Night of the Living Dead zombies. Sometimes Teeny remembers to cry, but usually she just lies there looking at her favorite blond-dead-grunge-rock star's chin and listening to the wind like his ghost and trying to think what it is that is gone.

Barbie would not have agreed to any more modeling work after New York, but her mother had persuaded her. It was an animal rights campaign that was going to be shot by the world-famous photographer Stephanie Mazer, who had gained notoriety from posing the most fascinating celebrities in the most unusual and soul-revealing ways. Starlets as mermaids, Hollywood hunks covered with leaves, politicians as circus performers. Barbie wanted to see how someone like Stephanie worked, especially if it might help a baby moose. And Mrs. Marks had said all the right things.

"I'm sorry if I haven't been the best mother. I really tried. I do want what's best for you. . . . I'm on your side. I've been thinking a lot about everything. If you don't want to do this campaign it's fine. But I thought it might mean something to you."

Barbie still said no. But when her mother showed her the list of people who were participating in the campaign, she thought again. Griffin Tyler. If Griffin had agreed it was probably a pretty special thing. And—not that I *care*, she told herself—but she might see Todd.

Mrs. Marks knew she had won. She lay back with a sigh and began to grease her thighs with suntan oil.

Barbie thought of Mab again. If she had been there she would never have let Barbie agree to do the shoot. But maybe it's better she's gone, Barbie thought. Maybe I'm growing up now. Maybe Mab was never real at all.

Then she remembered a story she had read when she was little. Something about belief and a girl like Mab. A perfect girl with wings and a singing name. And how, without the belief of the children, the girl like Mab would die.

Ashley Wells was squealing and wincing while a stylist attempted to drape a large king snake around her neck. When she saw Barbie she gave her a poisonous look, pushed away snake and stylist and slithered over.

"Hi, Barbie."

"Hi."

"Todd told me to tell you good luck on the shoot."

Barbie's heart felt dry and hollow. She realized with a thud in her chest that Todd was as much out of her life as Mab was—almost as if he had never been real at all. And someone like Todd—with his magic castle and his mythic beauty—seemed as much a fantasy creature as Mab did.

"How is he?" she asked Ashley.

"He's *excellent*," Ashley said nastily. "But then you'd know that, wouldn't you?"

"Not anymore."

"That's right. Not anymore."

Barbie turned away and noticed a boy slumped in a chair. Seeing him made her remember New York and Mab and Todd and it was all real again and she wanted to run over and kiss him. She just ran over, instead, with kissing eyes, and when he saw her his eyes kissed her back.

"Hey, Barbie."

"Griffin! I'm so glad you're here!" She squeezed his arm.

"You too."

"It's a cool cause. And Stephanie Mazer!"

"Yeah. I came out of retirement for it."

She grinned at him, remembering Todd saying how alike she and Griffin were.

Then she noticed that he was frowning at something over her shoulder. At first she thought—Ashley—but it was a stylist preparing a shot of a young boy with a baby lion.

"Is that safe?" Barbie asked.

"He's been de-clawed," the stylist said.

"I thought this was an animal rights thing."

The stylist shrugged. "The new photographer said he wanted it."

"I thought Stephanie Mazer was doing this," said Griffin.

The stylist was back at work arranging the boy and the cub. "She had something last minute. It's Hamilton Waverly."

Maybe it was self-preservation, or maybe it was love, or a little of both, but Barbie didn't think about anything at that moment except Griffin. She remembered how he had looked that day, so long ago, being dragged into the studio by his mother. At least she had had a Mab to talk to.

Hamilton Waverly walked into the room.

He hadn't aged much. He had less hair on top and the ponytail was gone, but his skin was the same—unlined and mushroomy. He wore a pair of trendy European glasses with sickly yellow lenses that looked too small for his face.

"This is looking great," he said, taking in the room full of teenagers and animals with a sweep of his pudgy hand. He kissed a few of the female assistants on their cheeks and shook hands with the men. Everyone seemed impressed by his expensive linen shirt and Italian leather pants. Barbie thought she might vomit into her purse.

She and Griffin watched as Hamilton Waverly made his rounds. He stopped at the young boy with the lion cub. The boy had tawny hair and round brown eyes like the lion. Hamilton Waverly discussed something with the stylist.

Barbie wanted to squeeze Griffin's hand, but she just stood there, watching, as helpless and paralyzed as the little girl who had not been able to run from the Cyclops eye of the camera five years ago.

By the time Griffin finally came to the door that night Barbie had started to walk away. She turned to see him standing under the carved angel, his face just as pale and sculpted-looking as its stone one.

"Hey. You're there. Can I come in?"

"Todd's not here," he mumbled, starting to back into the dim house.

Barbie had the shivery impression that a party of old-Hollywood ghosts were waiting for him to join them as they sipped their phantom dust-wine. But when she followed him inside there were no ghosts, not the kind that danced around old houses, anyway. Maybe the kind that lived in the heads of sad boys, though. The kind that made the boys drink very real alcohol by the bottle.

Barbie and Griffin were sharing one of Jack Daniel's, in front of the fireplace where she and Todd had made love that night. They're so different, Barbie thought, watching Griffin huddled up with his back against the sofa, his hair in his face, his delicate hand gripping the bottle.

"I need to know," she said.

He took a gulp of liquor and closed his eyes as it cut its way down his throat.

"Griffin?"

"Why are you asking me?" he said finally.

"Because I saw your face when you saw him."

He turned to her, scowling. She realized that he actually resembled Mab a little, especially

when he was mad. "What about my face?"
he said.

"You know, Griffin."

He looked into the empty fireplace again.
Shadows nestled in his cheekbones, as if in
love with them. "I don't want to talk about it."

Barbie was getting mad, too, now. She
thought of the little boy who looked like a toy
lion cub. "But we have to talk. He might be
still doing it."

Griffin didn't say anything.

"If I had told someone when it happened
to me it might have made him stop. He might
do it to that little boy today."

Griffin picked up his bong. He wished he
were small enough to climb inside it and be
submerged in pot smoke. He couldn't handle
this. Remembering. It would fuck him up for
good. "So you go tell someone," he said.

Barbie stood. He stared at her bony knees
in the striped thigh-high stockings and her
Fluevog shoes, pretending that she was a
Giant who could step on him, crush out all the
little waste of life that was Griffin Tyler.

"Fine, I will," she said. She started to
clomp away, then turned back. "I just thought
maybe you'd help me."

Griffin took a swig from the bottle of J.D. He lit the bong and had a hit. The ugly mushroom-colored, slack-lipped, balding ghosts kept spinning around inside of him, no matter how much alcohol or smoke he used to drive them out.

When Barbie got outside she saw Todd's candy black-and-pink convertible coming down the street toward her. It stopped but she kept walking, her heart racing faster than the old engine had revved before he killed it. Todd jumped out over the door like a stunt man.

"Wait, baby! What's up?"

"I was talking to Griffin," she said, still walking.

He grabbed her arm and pulled her to face him, then reached out to brush away a strand of hair that clung to the dampness on her flushed cheek. "Are you okay?"

"I'm fine. Ashley tells me you're just fine, too."

Todd shook his head. The sunlight through the trees was dappling his face with green and golden leaves of light. "I had lunch with her last week. That's all."

Barbie looked away.

"You wouldn't see me!"

She made a face that felt very Mablike, twisted and bitter.

"I am so crazy about you! Don't do this to me. Tell me what's going on."

He said it with so much real feeling that she almost believed it less; that was the trouble with good actors. But she wasn't an actor. She could fake a face but not words. If she could, she would have said, "Chill out, Todd. I am so over you." Instead she said the real ones. "Everyone I've ever trusted has fucked with me. Or left."

Todd leaned nearer so she could see two girls, the size of Mab, shining in his dark eyes. She wished she were those girls.

Everyone I've ever really trusted has fucked with me. Or left.

"Well, not me," Todd said.

And when he put his arms around her, she felt like the girls in his eyes, safe inside of him, all he could see.

Griffin stared at his reflection in the window, an outline of a young man whose body was full of night.

He had been awakened by the dream. In it he was a little boy holding a kitten. Bright lights flashed on and off in his eyes. Noises slammed his ears. The lights were noise and the noises were lights. He cuddled closer to the kitten, as if it could protect him.

The boots stomped over, echoing. They stopped in front of him.

"Nice kitty. Here kitty kitty," the man said.

And then the kitten changed. Bursting out like something from a horror movie, its lion-self ripping from it, clawing and roaring. Not to protect him. It turned and opened its jaws as Griffin tried to scream.

He was still clammy from fear as he stood at the window. "You're a fucking coward," he said to his see-through, night-filled twin. "You're afraid, because you think that if you tell what he did they'll all know about you."

He stopped and pressed his burning forehead against the chilly pane. "Maybe it was your fault he did what he did. Maybe you encouraged him to do it because you like men."

The window shifted slightly under the pressure of his head and he pushed it all the way open. He leaned toward the night that was already so deep inside him.

"Hey," he called to it, "hey, little chick thing with the wings! Hey, Miss Pesky, or whatever you are. I'm a fairy, too! Hey, I'm a freaking fairy too."

He hoisted himself up onto the window ledge and held on to the top of the frame, his body swaying forward over the sidewalk that tilted beneath him.

"Hey! Remember how you taught me to fly? Maybe I should try it without you. After all, I'm a fairy too."

Griffin wasn't scared anymore. He didn't even feel sad, really. Very calm. Like everything had led him to this, this moment, and it was where he was supposed to be. The ghosts, stoned now on J.D. and pot, were whispering, telling him he was doing the right thing. What was the use of staying? Not only did he have his pain still; he hadn't been able to do anything with it for someone else.

If Griffin had seen Barbie and Todd pull up just then, maybe he would have changed his mind. If he had seen the expressions on their faces. He was the kind of person that couldn't have done it if he had seen what it would do to them.

It is hard to say what really happened. Maybe Griffin did see Barbie and Todd and never leapt at all. Or maybe he didn't see them. Maybe he let go of the window and was released into the night that was already inside of him.

Maybe Griffin felt Todd and Barbie's love like a sparkling web of light spinning around him. Or maybe the web of light was there after he leapt, singing in a high voice about coming away, to waters and to wild, away from the weeping that he could not understand.

"Hey!" Griffin said, maybe to Mab.

"Hey, yourself," she sniffed.

"What are you doing here?"

"What am *I* doing? What are you doing? I do this all the time. I told you not to try it without my supervision."

"How'd you get here so fast?"

"I heard you call. Although I don't usually respond to 'chick thing' or 'Miss Pesky.'"

"Sorry."

"Do not say sorry. Ever again. I hate that. Unless it is coming out of the mouths of crocodile pedophile slime balls." She scowled so that even he recognized the similarity of their faces in mad mode. "Actually, I didn't hear you call. I was just getting a little homesick. I hitched a ride from Manhattan on the back of this stupid pigeon. At least I didn't get airsick."

And maybe then Mab flew Griffin back to the ledge. He stepped into the room and leaned out toward her, a tiny greenish star. She was . . . what was she . . . there was a word, he couldn't . . .

"You are a total biscuit, by the way," she said.

And Griffin saw the stone carving on the side of the hotel, the one with the wings, much bigger than Mab but still . . . and then he knew. "And you're an angel," Griffin said.

Mab made an annoyed sound in her throat. "Please! What a bore!" But she twinkled more brightly for a moment. "Well, see you around, biscuit. And don't try anything like that again in this lifetime."

"Good. Night," Griffin whispered, as if she were the night itself. And then, that was all that was left of her.

Griffin was collapsed on the bed when Todd and Barbie burst through the door. He did not flinch from the warmth of their bodies when they flung themselves on top of him, as if protecting him from gunfire.

There is a very famous story about a boy who knew someone a lot like Mab. But in that story, the boy saved her life by getting the children to believe in her. In *this* one, Griffin thought, the Mab taught the boy to believe in himself.

There was another boy Mab needed to visit. As soon as she left Griffin, she flew west to the area commonly known as Boys' Town.

Mab tried to imagine how it would be if all these boys were fairies in the real sense, like her. I'd have quite the life, she thought. As it was, however, she could only hope to be queen of the queens and that was iffy, since none of them were going to get to see her.

Well, all but one, that is. Mab had already carefully chosen him on her way back from New York. It had taken her a whole night of searching in West Hollywood, which for her was a long time since she had such a savvy sense of matchmaking. She could have gone into business as a matchmaker if she'd chosen to do it, but wouldn't because she didn't care enough about most people to bother with their desperate searchings.

This wasn't the case with Griffin. Mab knew he needed someone to get his mind off his sexual angst and his interest in that silly roommate of his. She had spotted Damian finally, near dawn, as he was leaving the nightclub where he worked as a go-go boy. He was part Asian with light-green slanted eyes and that black-mirror hair, dripping with sweat from his gyrations. Although he worked as a dancer, Mab discovered by going through his backpack that Damian Chen was an art student at the local college, that he was HIV$^-$, twenty years old, had a good relationship with his parents to whom he had come out, (this, revealed in a letter they'd sent from Sacramento asking if he'd met any nice boys yet) and was searching for his true love (this, revealed in a diary entry: "Where are you my wingless but ascending angel?"). Mab thought he was certainly lovely enough for Griffin and she liked his sketches for school very much. Looks, talent, taste, intelligence, good upbringing, good heart, good health. He'd do. Plus, he had a noticeable resemblance to a certain dark-haired hetero heart-throb who lived in

what she believed was a too-close proximity
to her young Griff.

That night, Mab returned to the club to
find Damian the human gyroscope pulling off
his sweaty T-shirt in one great swoop like a
bird taking flight. She buzzed around him for a
while, trying to get a better sense of him,
sniffing his hair, tasting his skin, before making her move. Finally she settled in his ear
and began tickling him until he had to take a
break and step outside, scratching at his neck.
She was pleased to see he wasn't a smoker or
a drinker but gulped heartily from a bottle of
mineral water.

Damian, despite his well-adjusted back-
ground, had had his share of "the crock," as
Mab called it, although he'd mostly forgotten
about the thing that had happened when he
was eight. Sometimes he still dreamed about
it, though—the way they held him down and
took turns with him, calling him a faggot—
and when a boyfriend touched him in a certain
way, he'd get paralyzed with fear for no appar-
ent reason. Because of this, Damian was quite
able to see Mab when she came to him, and to
accept her almost immediately. He was an art
student also, after all, and the possibilities of

her impact on his creative vision were thrilling.

He hadn't expected her to be Miss Matchmaker, however.

"Mr. Damian Chen," Mab said, holding up the page from his diary that she had snagged the night before, "I have found your wingless and ascending one."

When Barbie stomped into the room like a warrior in engineer boots Mrs. Marks was watching an info-mercial for an abs machine on the TV. She glanced up briefly from her martini and spat the olive back into the glass.

"I want to talk to you," Barbie said.

"Hmmm?" said her mother. Her face was florid from sun and the drink. Her mascara was running in blue streaks.

"Please turn off the TV."

Mrs. Marks rolled her eyes and hit the remote button to turn down the sound but kept glancing at the picture on the screen. The model's abdominal muscles rippled sleekly.

"What is it?" Mrs. Marks slurred. Her eyes had an uncanny, fizzy brightness like television screens.

"You usually stay around for the shoots."

"I had some errands to do, I told you. Besides, I thought you were sick of me."

"You never worried about that before," Barbie said. "Do you know who the photographer was?"

Mrs. Marks shrugged and took another sip. "That Stephanie-something woman that you like so much."

"Well, it wasn't. Can you guess who it was?"

"What are you talking about?"

Barbie turned off the TV and stood in front of the still-hot screen. "It was Hamilton Waverly. Remember? Old Ham? That nice man that took my picture when I was a little girl?"

Mrs. Marks sat up and fanned her face with her fingernails.

"And that's not all he took from me," Barbie said.

"Just calm down," said her mother.

"And you knew! You knew what he did and you didn't protect me. And we let it keep going."

"I didn't know anything." Mrs. Marks sucked up the last of her drink from the bottom of her glass. Her eyes darted frantically around—TV screen, bar—seeking something to help her. All she found was her unkempt, hollow-eyed daughter. "And besides," she said, "what could I have done? We had our career to think about."

The fury exploded then, in Barbie, like a whole army of mad Mabs flying out of her chest. She didn't know what she said, only that every word was a Mab aiming a dagger at her mother. When she was through she ran upstairs, locked the door and played Wig Starbuck's *Eat Your World* so loud that she could not hear the sobs coming from the living room.

Minutes before midnight, after Mrs. Marks was passed out over another tear-salted martini, Barbie was throwing a pair of skinny baby-blue damask pants into her suitcase when she heard a chirping sound outside her window. She went to look out at the bird cage that she had left on the moist lawn. It was there as a kind of welcome message to Mab, whom she kept hoping might some day fly past, see it, and be moved to return for good. Of course, it won't work, Barbie told herself. Mab always hated that bird cage any-way. But who was chirping? Maybe Emily had come back. She wasn't Mab, but Barbie missed her, too. And besides, Emily talked back in a much more pleasant fashion.

When she got down into the garden, with her suitcase, she saw that it was indeed Emily the parakeet sitting inside the cage. Barbie almost squealed like a baby when she saw her. Emily cocked her head as if she were looking at something behind her former mistress's shoulder.

"Emily?" Barbie said.

"That pigeon of yours isn't such a bad little mode of transportation."

"Mab?" said Barbie. She almost couldn't bring herself to look around. What if this time she learned that it really was just a voice in her head? Maybe there had never really been . . .

A flickering light. "Thank you for coming back," Barbie said, trying to contain herself, trying to keep from shouting she was sorry or, even worse, attempting to kiss the bright bit of air hovering so near her lips.

"It's just temporary," Mab said, cool as the green of her eyes.

Barbie tried to imitate the chill. "How's New York?"

"Fabulous!"

It was said with just a tiny bit too much enthusiasm, Barbie thought. "Have you had your pictures taken yet?"

Mab shrugged her fragile shoulders so that her wings lifted up. Seeing them made Barbie's chest tighten. "Oh that," Mab said.

"Because if not then I'd really like to do it. I think we could make you into the new It Girl."

Mab examined her fingernails which, Barbie noticed, were not stained with flower juice as usual, but a little ragged and dirty. "I've always been It," she said. Then she added, in a softer voice, ". . . If you insist."

A car horn honked and Barbie jumped up. "That's Todd. Come on!" She motioned for Mab to fly into the cage with Emily.

It was maybe the first time she had ever told—rather than asked—Mab to do something. Mab hesitated for a moment, eyeing Barbie, Emily, the cage. She was caught off guard by this assertive behavior. Maybe some of the therapy had started to work. Well, it looked like the pigeon was finally leaving the crocodile. She decided she'd go along for the ride, just to do a case study, of course.

Besides, the biscuit was there.

Of course, Mab didn't have the opportunity to make out with him the whole trip, the way Todd and Barbie were doing, *quite insensitively*, she thought. She had to stay hidden in the stinky cage, next to the little pigeon or whatever it was, who kept cocking its silly head at her as if to say, "Remember, I got you here. Shouldn't you express a little gratitude? Aren't I the cutest thing you've ever seen?"

Mab cocked her head at Emily and stuck out her tongue, knowing that Miss Bird could not even begin to imitate the second gesture.

The next morning Barbie woke in Todd's arms. Emily was chirping love songs in the cage, with Mab sleeping cuddled beside her, and sunlight was filtering through the gauze draperies like a beam of kisses. Barbie slipped out of bed and into one of Todd's T-shirts. She stretched, feeling long, sinewy, calm as a kitty cat.

While she was downstairs making blueberry banana pancakes for Todd and Griffin, the phone rang. She let the machine answer; it was Griffin's agent with a message that the shoot had been canceled for the day *but where the hell did you go yesterday and you better get back to me.*

Barbie flipped the last pancake off the griddle and into the oven to stay warm. Why was it canceled? She thought about the lion cub boy and the way Hamilton Waverly had looked at him. Even the memory of Todd's love in her body, the burnt sugar smell of the pancakes, the knowledge that Mab was back, didn't make it better.

She went upstairs and tiptoed into Todd's room to dress. In the bird cage Mab was—miraculously—still asleep although Emily hadn't stopped chirping. Barbie opened the cage and poked Mab with her pinkie.

Mab woke, saw the "pigeon" she was leaning against, made a disgusted face, brushed herself off, scowled at Barbie. "What?" she said.

Mab was not a morning girl. She needed a good strong dose of honeysuckle and a few hours of peace and quiet to get into gear. Plus it hadn't been a good night with all that incessant chirping; it was a wonder she had been able to sleep at all.

Barbie held a finger to her lips and gestured for Mab to follow her. Before she left the room she grabbed a Polaroid camera from Todd's Adam and Eve cabinet.

So Mab and Barbie like Batman and Robin before them (although only the bravest of souls would have ventured to ask who was who) embarked on their adventure in Todd's Continental, the smaller of the partners riding on the dashboard.

When people pulled up beside them, Mab would stop hopping around and remain as still as possible like a dashboard doll ornament. But when she saw the billboard of Ashley, lying prone and twisted like an accident victim, she could not resist flipping it off, even though a man in the car beside them was leaning his head out the window to look at her. Mab resumed her stationary pose and Barbie tore off down the street. She would have laughed if their journey was not of such a serious nature.

They went to the photo studio first. It was empty except for the woman at the desk and a few ominously cute stuffed animals scattered around the floor. The woman looked up from filing her fingernails.

"Didn't they call you?" she asked Barbie. "The shoot's been canceled."

"I wasn't at home. Do you know where Waverly is?"

"He's at his place. He wanted to do some work with one of the kids"—but the woman's last words might as well have been uttered to the stuffed giraffe on the floor by her feet; Barbie was already out the door.

Barbie and Mab did not resemble your typical superheroes. Both were too small; one was unusually small. Possibly, if she had pursued it, and gotten breast implants, the taller one might have had the chance to be a supermodel. The other had supernatural wings. Otherwise there was nothing particularly super about either of them. But together they were heroes.

Mab flew up to the window at the back of Hamilton Waverly's studio. She looked in and gestured down to Barbie who was waiting on the street below.

Barbie twisted her hair back into a ponytail, rolled up her extra-long Levi's and hoisted herself onto the fire escape.

Inside the studio Hamilton Waverly was photographing the little lion boy.

Hamilton Waverly had never meant to hurt Barbie or Griffin or any of the others. He did not mean to hurt the lion boy. At first it was okay. He could just look at them through the camera and not need anymore. They were captured there for him and he didn't need anything else. He had them alone in the dark-room—the images of them with their trusting eyes and mouths. No one got hurt.

But then later, the longing began. It was only to comfort them. They were all so sad. Their parents throwing them into the lights for money like circus freaks. No one ever seemed to ask them what they felt about it all. He wanted to listen to them. He wanted to know what was inside of them, too; not just to take their beauty.

But then he found that he could not get inside the way he needed to. And the longing began to tear at him like a wild creature in the cage of his body. And things happened before he could stop himself.

Then he would have to threaten them so they wouldn't tell. That was the worst part of all. He didn't want them to be afraid. But if they weren't made afraid, more afraid, even, than of the idea of having to live with the secret, he would lose everything. He would never get to comfort another one again.

Hamilton Waverly moved closer to the little boy. Shooting shot after shot. Leaning all the way in. The eyes looked up at him, widening, just at the edge of the moment when the trust would turn to confusion and then fear.

Hamilton hated that moment. He wanted the eyes to stay trusting. At least he had that look captured in his camera. He dropped it and put his hand on the boy's leg. It always surprised him how fragile they felt, like you could break them in two and make a wish.

That was when he heard his camera going off by itself, again and again. It seemed like his camera. But then he realized, no, it was coming from the window behind him. And he heard his name.

"Hey! Waverly!"

He turned and saw the hooded figure at the window. He might have seen the Mab on her shoulder, too, and remembered how once he had had a Mab—a shadow-winged creature to whom he told what his stepfather had done to him. But any memory that might have returned was lost; Barbie and Mab were gone, down the fire escape.

Lion-boy's mother and father were pacing back and forth in front of the studio. The father kept rolling up his sleeve, checking his watch, rolling down his sleeve. Suddenly, he saw a girl in baggy clothes running up to him. She was holding something out—a Polaroid photo. Before he had even examined it, he pushed on the front door with his shoulder and began shouting until Hamilton Waverly came down to let him in.

Griffin was lying on his bed looking at a photo of himself and his mother from when he was little. His mother looked too young to have a five-year-old kid. She had the smile of a sixteen-year-old and a light coming out of her. Griffin hardly saw her anymore. She had married some rich plastic surgeon and moved to Santa Barbara.

Griffin had never told his mom about what had happened to him. He'd never told anyone, not even that shrink she brought him

to, who kept asking why he seemed so uncomfortable in his body. Maybe if he'd told,
he'd have felt different. Or maybe someone
else would have been able to escape what happened to him. Like that little boy.

There was a knock on the door.

"Can I come in?" Barbie asked.

"It's open."

She came and sat on a chair by the window. Griffin thought she seemed different, but
he couldn't figure out why. She seemed
stronger or something.

"How are you feeling?" she asked him.

Maybe it was because he'd been looking at
the picture of his mom, but the way Barbie
asked sounded hushed and maternal to him
and he relaxed a little. He'd thought she was
still mad at him.

"I'm okay," he said. "I wanted to talk to
you about something."

She waited, trying not to stare.

"Did you tell anyone yet?"

"It's all taken care of," Barbie said softly,
as if she were stroking his hair out of his
eyes the way his mother used to do. "I let the
parents know."

"Because if you need me . . ."

"We just need you to feel better."

Griffin glanced at the photo of himself, a beautiful boy with sensual lips and out-stretched arms. "I've always felt like it was my fault."

"But it wasn't!" Barbie got up and came to sit next to him on the bed. "It happened to me, too, Griffin. And it almost happened to that kid. You didn't do anything! You were just a little boy."

He realized that she was talking to herself at the same time. And he believed her, about both of them. The tears started to tickle his nose. He fought them back.

"Sorry. . . ." he said.

Barbie put her arms around his delicate back. "Never say that, Mr. Biscuit."

Biscuit? Where'd she get that word? Griffin looked at Barbie with shock (there was a Mab?) and with relief (a Mab there was!).

"It's all about belief," Mab said. "They create a mind-set where I, for instance, am un-believable. And they make you believe in 'they.' What is 'they' anyway? 'They' is a conceit they have created. There really is no 'they,' at least not a 'they' that has any authority. I am much more real than their 'they.' Do you follow me?"

Barbie nodded. "Now be quiet for a second or I'll never get this shot."

They were in Todd's courtyard, where Mab was posed on a large banana leaf, with a paper parasol and a maraschino cherry, while Barbie photographed her. Suddenly, through the lens, Barbie saw something that made her heart flutter like Mab's wings. She dropped the camera from her face and looked at the thing she'd thought she'd seen, sitting on the banana leaf next to Mab and kissing her hand.

"Why not?" Mab said. "If you believe in me . . ."

And she gestured for Barbie to snap a picture . . .

Of Mab. And the tiny red-haired boy with wings.

When Barbie looked back, he was gone. But she knew she'd seen him. At least as much as she knew she'd known Mab almost half her life. And she might have them both on film.

"Who is he?" she asked Mab. "He's cute."

"Cute? He's the biscuit king! He's from

Ireland. He came here via wild goose to be discovered." She paused and then grinned so wide that her sharp incisors showed against her lips. "And let me tell you, I've *discovered* him!"

Later, in Todd's room, Barbie held up the picture she had developed, staring at the pinwheels of light flaring out behind the two tiny figures on the leaf. So not only did Mab show up on film—she really wasn't the only one, after all.

But then why was she pacing back and forth over the covers as if something had upset her? She finally had what she'd always wanted, didn't she?

"What's wrong?" Barbie asked.

Mab flew up close to the photograph. "Do you think they'll think it's a fake?"

"That will be okay. It will cause controversy. You'll still be famous."

"If it gets published."

"It will."

Barbie was no longer afraid of anything. It was like the thing Mab had said about belief. The belief is sometimes the biggest part of it all. You can choose to believe in your published book being held in the loving hands of strangers, your name tattooed forever on the heart of the one you adore; you can choose to believe in tiny red-haired pesky piskies—all the things "they" may tell you not to believe in. But who are they anyway? What do they know? What makes them any more real? And now, Barbie realized, I am telling Mab to believe. I am telling Belief herself to believe.

That was when Barbie Marks knew she had changed into Selena Moon.

And she was right. The book was published. On the night it came out she wore a dress of silver fabric as sheer, shimmery, and breathless on her skin as Mab's wings. Todd leaned over to kiss her glitter-dusted cheek.

"Congratulations, baby," he said. "On everything."

She looked into his eyes. They were no longer matinée idol eyes, dark and mysterious as the movie theater before the show comes on, before the story is revealed. They were the eyes of her love biscuit—she knew their story. And she wanted to slip into them even more now that she did.

They drove past Hamilton Waverly's studio. There was a FOR RENT sign in the window and graffiti across the door that read, HAMILTON WAVERLY IS A CROCODILE PEDOPHILE.

"Can I ask you something?" Todd said.

She nodded, knowing what was coming. She was surprised he hadn't asked before.

"I knew you'd be a good photographer, but what technique did you use for those shots? They look so real?"

Barbie/Selena Moon considered telling him the whole story. But in a way it was beside the point now.

Whatever Mab had represented—Selena Moon had it all inside her now. And, whether they believed that the pictures were real or enhanced, all the people that would look at them and see a winged girl as tremulous and small and powerful as the beat of a heart had it inside them now, too.

Todd and Selena Moon pulled up in front of the bookstore. Teenyboppers with shaved heads and silver nose rings, lanky models, boyish actors in baseball caps and baggy jeans, black leather scenesters and gay gentlemen in neat sweaters were cramming the sidewalk, the overflow of the inside crowd.

"Hey, look who's here!" Todd said, pointing to two boys on a motorcycle who had pulled up behind them.

It was Griffin and a friend who resembled a slightly younger, thinner, less grungified, part-Asian Todd. Selena Moon squeezed Todd's hand. She was suddenly shy, like she didn't want to leave the car. He kissed her again and hopped out to open the door. By the time he got there, Griffin and the Todd look-alike had joined him.

"This is Damian Chen," said Griffin and, they shook the Todd-look-alike's hand.

Then all three gentlemen bowed and winked at Selena Moon before escorting her inside.

After Selena Moon had signed so many copies of her book, I Was a Teenage Fairy, that her wrist ached and her eyes swirled, after she had smiled mysteriously so often at the question, "How did you do it?" that her cheeks felt permanently dimpled, she looked up and saw her mother holding one last copy.

They had spoken only once since Selena

Moon had moved out. Selena Moon had called to say that she was safe and would not be returning home. When Mrs. Marks began to scream into the phone, her daughter had hung up. She had been a little surprised, and in a strange way slightly let down, that her mother didn't pursue it after that.

When Barbie's book was published, Mrs. Marks, who had lost touch with her daughter for so long, rushed out to get a copy. After studying it for a while, she was disturbed by feelings so powerful that she had been compelled to rummage around in her jewelry box for the number of a psychotherapist she had met years ago at a party with her ex-husband.

She called, set up an appointment, and brought the book into the therapist's office. The woman, a tall redhead with a delicious laugh and compassionate eyes, merrily examined *I Was a Teenage Fairy* (the Mab in it had a striking resemblance, she thought privately, to herself as a young and at the time less compassionate girl, although of course much more petite) and asked Mrs. Marks how it made her feel.

"It's so strange, but when I was a girl I think . . . I think it's just so familiar to me. I don't know what tricks she used but the part that is really strange to me is how much it looks like . . . I don't know."

"I believe you do," the therapist said, smiling but with eyes just sad enough that Mrs. Marks did not feel as if she were being made fun of.

And Mrs. Marks did begin to remember; there were tiny wings of pain stirring in her chest.

"Bad things happen," she said quickly. "You just go on. That's what I told myself."

She had said it for so long that the stirring had stopped. If she allowed it to be real then the bad thing that had brought it would also have to be real and so it had been necessary to forget them both. But here it was again—the stirring—very like a Mab inside of her. She put her hand to her chest.

The therapist nodded. "I knew you'd know," the therapist said.

Now Mrs. Marks put the book down on the table and brought a huge bouquet of peachy roses tied with metallic ribbon out from behind her back.

"I'm so proud of you," she said. "You finally have achieved the fame you deserve."

Mab might have objected to the speed with which Barbie accepted the roses and forgave her mother without even bringing up the Hamilton Waverly betrayal or questioning Mrs. Marks's motives for wanting to patch things up at that time. She might have spat or bit or at least shouted obscenities, thereby providing proof that the photographs were not fakes in any way and securing her fame, and the fame of Selena Moon. But Mab was too busy to cause a scene. She and her winged biscuit were furiously making love and trying not to accidentally ascend with euphoria out of the safe dark perfumed haven of Barbie's turquoise satin purse.

Selena Moon lay on Todd's four poster bed, feeling the white gauze draperies blowing against her burning face and watching the candle flames blur through her tears. Todd's body inside of hers was startling and tender at once, completely different and an exact extension of who she was. His rhythms were transporting her—she couldn't tell if what she was seeing was an orgasmic hallucination from the lovemaking, or real.

Mab and her red-haired friend were suspended in the air behind Todd's T-shirted torso. They wore tiny backpacks situated carefully between their wings.

"What are you doing?" Selena Moon asked.

"What? I hope you can tell," said Todd.

Mab held up a sign that read *Going to Ireland. Thanks for everything. And remember—do everything I would do!* She flipped the sign over. *Sorry to bother you mid-biscuit-bake session, but we have to go.*

"Never say sorry for stuff like that," Selena Moon whispered to the candle-lit, gauzy, tear-blurred air. "I love you."

Mab winked at her and Selena Moon winked back. Todd cocked his head in confusion, just like Emily and her new beau, Joseph, who had been necking intensely on the perch of their nearby cage.

"I'm not sure what's going on. But I love you, too, Selena Moon."

And then Todd pulled his shirt up over his

head. Selena Moon cringed for a second—it was an unspoken thing between them that he never revealed his bare tattooed chest.

But now the tattoo was different. SARAH, LISA, and NINA had lost some letters under a camouflage of inky flowers and been combined, E's added, into the name SELENA.

And of course, the FOREVER remained.

Selena Moon kissed Todd Forever as Mab and her friend flew out the window. But Mab had not finished her good-byes. On the street in front of the hotel Griffin and Damian were standing by the motorcycle talking. Mab flew down and circled them in her light-web. Maybe webs of light are just a feeling two people have when they are in love. Maybe webs of light are really from Mabs. Either way, Griffin and Damian felt something binding them together in the darkness.

Maybe Mab was real. Maybe she was the fury, the courage, the sex. Whatever Mab had been, now, joined with her tiny winged red-haired biscuit, Mab was the love, flying through night like an errant star that had longed to know, even briefly, what made planet Earth's children weep and sing.